PERDUE

A Marie Perdita Suspense

ALSO BY CHARLES D'AMICO

<u>Neil Baggio Suspense Series</u>

VERITAS

AVE MARIA

COLLOQUIUM

REQUIEM

<u>Standalone novels</u>

ONE GOLDEN DAY

PRAISE FOR PERDUE

"Marie proves a superb hero... With exciting showdowns, D'Amico brings the reader into the vibrant world of New Orleans."

— *PUBLISHERS WEEKLY*

"Perdue is a firecracker of a thriller that had me biting fingernails and turning pages so fast—I finished reading in a single day. The story centers on Marie, a strong and saucy spy with smarts and guts galore."

— *SARALYN RICHARD, author of the award-winning Detective Parrott Mystery Series*

"New lead, new angle, same excellent writing. Another page-turning mastery from Charles D'Amico."

— *ANDREW J BRANDT, bestselling author of Picture Unavailable and Palo Duro*

PERDUE

A Marie Perdita Suspense

Charles D'Amico

@Charles3Hats

(All Social)

Blue Handle Publishing
Amarillo, Texas

Copyright © 2022 Charles D'Amico
All rights reserved, including the right to reproduce this book or any portions thereof in any form whatsoever. For information, address: Blue Handle Publishing 2607 Wolflin #963 Amarillo, TX 79109

For information about bulk, educational and other special discounts, please contact Blue Handle Publishing.

Cover & Interior Design: Blue Handle Publishing, L.L.C

Editing: Book Puma Editorial Services
BookPumaOnline.com

BOOK PUMA

ISBN: 978-1-7347727-7-7

For all those who have stuck with me through this
journey:

My loving, supportive wife;
My mother looking down on me;
and the literary inspiration, whom I wish to write
one hundred books for — my sister.

1

"Focus on the reward, not the fear. I can do that."

W here do I start? You may know me from the escapades I have had with BCI, Neil Baggio, and Gaines Chemical. Luckily for this girl, I'm an asset my country wants to use; otherwise, I'd still be a burned spy or in a dark prison somewhere. But I've also done some unforgivable things; I have killed an FBI agent, plus a witness for a crime boss, one that friends were close to putting away for a long time. I fell into a trap, and climbing out of that dark hole put me in the crosshairs of some bad people.

When the CIA brought me back in, they told me I needed to change my name again, so the new and hopefully improved me is known as Marie Perdita. Marie reminds me of the last person who ever trusted me, someone very close to my heart, so I felt it was a great place to begin.

My new first name had to be something I'll feel normal and familiar with over time. And I thought *perdita* was a bit funny since it's Latin for lost. Plus, the name Marie Perdita looks superb when I sign it; it's the little things that get us through the day. Since I've had to change who I am over and over, this is a way for me to feel at home despite feeling lost.

My name was Erin Beddington, but I've gone by so many last names that I don't know who I am anymore.

What I do know is that Erin is the name I was born with. It was also my grandmother's name.

But that's not important right now.

What *is* important is that I'm on a riverboat riding up the Mississippi outside of New Orleans, my hands bound with tape and a gag in my mouth. I'm being left for dead in a pile of trash, but this can't be the end for me.

But before I explain how I got here, let me give you a little background on where I'm from.

I grew up in the small town of Rincon, Georgia, to a farmer father and three brothers. I'm the second oldest. For my family's sake and the safety of all involved, I'll keep their names out of it, but I will share some stories that got me to this point.

Growing up in that small town allowed us the small-town feel with access to a city much bigger nearby. Though Savannah isn't like Atlanta, it feels huge compared to Rincon. That family life, living on a farm, taught me the value of hard work and shit days. Life is going to throw rough weeks at you; that's just the way it is. You're going to have poor crop seasons and have to live broke. That mindset, along with my drive and intellect, have allowed me to survive this long on a career path not known for longevity.

Having three bigger brothers, even though I was older than two of them, gave me a bit of a complex. I was super aggressive in sports, always trying to outdo my siblings. There I was (and still am) standing a mere five-seven and weighing in at about one-forty. My brothers, though, were all more than six feet and played football like proper country southern boys. One of them, the middle brother, got into baseball because of a coach and now plays in the majors. They didn't care that I was a girl.

I was a three-sport athlete, specializing in running. I was a cross-country and track star, even at the state level. Then I played basketball for fun and to stay in shape. I was always pushing myself to do better, and I took the same approach with school. My mother, an English professor at the local college, made certain of that. She was always my motivator with school. Even as a spy, I want to make my mother proud, yet she can never know what I do.

My family thinks I joined the military and do secret research projects for Homeland Security. It covers me being gone for months at a time, sometimes longer. I know it's hard on them, but it's a dream that I had to chase. My father is a Marine. After serving for almost a decade, he retired at twenty-seven. When he met my mother, he became a farmer and settled down. He outworked, outhustled, and out-loved everyone I knew. I think it's safe to say my fearless attitude came from watching him wake at four in the morning and push for that success in everything.

I can remember the day that it all came to fruition, the day that fear no longer stopped me. I was struggling to swing off a rope into the lake next to our property. The swing was on an embankment nearly ten feet above the lake. This meant a pretty big drop, especially for an eleven-year-old still afraid of heights. My dad pulled me aside when he watched me struggling, with my mom screaming in the background.

"Honey, if she doesn't want to swing, don't force her!" my mom yelled.

"Erin, you eventually have to learn to embrace your fears. Life is going to be filled with them. If you don't want to do something because it's not fun for you, that's one thing. Don't let fear stop you from enjoying something. Fear is just an awareness that something different is happening. It's up to you to manage it, sift through the variables, and make a decision." That's how my dad talked—Marine, remember?

"Dad, it's not that simple. You don't know how scared I am right now."

"Baby girl, I'm not fearless. Hell, I'm scared shitless plenty. The only difference is I don't let it stop me. Now you can sit here, give up, and wonder 'what if.' This is a defining moment in your character. This can be the step forward for the next ten years."

"I know, Dad. I want to be strong, and I want to be fearless."

"It's not about being fearless. It's about wanting the reward on the other side of fear more. That's what you need to focus on. Focus on the fun you'll have, the excitement you'll have every time you come out here once you overcome this fear."

"Focus on the reward, not the fear. I can do that."

I grabbed the rope and thought about all the fun my brothers were having. My younger brother was only eight and he was flying off this thing like he's a pro. That smile he gets, the joy I see in his face, I want that. No, I need that. Dad is right.

I took a couple of deep breaths, got all psyched up, sprinted down the hill a bit, and took off. I had gone so fast I spun my little body to the point that I did a somersault in the air, landing in the water feet-first. When I came up for air, I could hear my brothers and Dad screaming and clapping for me. You would have thought I just won the state championship with that jump.

"Hell yeah, girl, that's it! Don't let anything stop you ever again!" Dad was going nuts.

"Sis, you rock! Did you see that flip?!"

"I didn't see it; I was too busy doing it. Hell, yeah!" We high-fived and screamed a bit.

"Aren't you glad you did that now?"

"Heck yeah. That was AWESOME!"

It was that day, that moment in my life, that changed it all. The course of my life could have gone in an entirely different direction had my father not stepped in and coached me. Without that guidance, without that phrase in my head, I can see so many choices I made coming out differently. *Focus on the reward past the fear* rings in my ears all the time.

One could also say that's the first step in the journey that led to me stuck on a riverboat with no backup, doing off-book jobs for the CIA because of other poor choices in my life. I was asked to look into a lead involving a local crew into everything from drug running to major theft. They have recently been accused of upping their game to weapons trafficking. The CIA wants to know if they are terrorists or simply in it for the money.

Remember that part where I told you I came back to the CIA? It's only half true. I know I'm lying already, but what can I say? It's a habit; it's a reflex at this point in my life. They brought me back, but they ship me out to other agencies for cases such as this. Don't think of me as a hired gun in the wild west or some futuristic crime-fighting movie. Whatever awesome role you are imagining, I'm not it. I'm more like a really talented retail worker getting thrown around during the holiday season to do the shittiest jobs around. The only difference is that these window sets could quite possibly get me killed. My government figured instead of throwing me away in a dark hole, they'd use my skills for their purposes. I get to stay out of prison and get to do what I love. They get someone willing to take crazy risks to stay out of prison, like encouraging large men to hit me as a way to distract them.

"She isn't going to tell us shit. This Ms. Perdita lady is crazy. We might as well kill her now." The

Cajun accent is a bit thick, but I can understand it.

"Hey guys, don't be talking dirty in front of the lady; that's not nice." I need to buy some time.

"Just do us a favor and either tell us where you hid our money or shut up!" He's so macho.

"Aren't we Mr. Macho Guy, getting all big in front of the little lady?"

He reared back and hit me one more time, a nasty cross. Shit, that hurt. It felt like my face exploded for a minute. I intended to get him angry, hoping he either breaks the chair or does something stupid. Like, oh shit, here we go.

"Ms. Perdita, shut up! Just stop your incessant talking or I'll throw you overboard." I knew he couldn't throw me that far, weak-ass!

"Twenty bucks says you can't get me clear of the lower deck. If you throw me, chair and all, I'll crash below."

He picked me up quite easily; this might not have been a good idea. He lifted me up above his head and tossed me over the railing. That shit was so fast that before I knew it, I was crashing down into the water. Although, not before the chair and my legs caught the side of the boat, breaking it up just enough that I could get free. Well, this should be fun; now I have to free my hands so I can swim to shore. I never was a fan of my father's crazy survival tests, but in moments like this, I get all nostalgic.

I know, right? You had no idea what you were getting yourself into.

2

"I left you alone on that boat for three minutes…"

I n the summer before I turned fourteen, my father thought I was old enough to start doing survival training. If my mom only knew the crazy shit he had us do; then again, I got it worse than my brothers. He used to tell me the world is hard on women and I needed to be twice as tough as them. I used to think he was nuts, but now I can take a punch or get thrown off a riverboat and survive. Thanks, Dad: You're one crazy dude, but I love you. My father did multiple tours in some messed-up places. He's seen some shit; it's given him the values and perceptions he carries to this day.

So, there I was, July 4th weekend before high school. I should have been worrying about boys or pimples, anything other than survival training. I mean, who teaches their kids this shit? Marines do. Navy SEALs do. I know this because that was my dad's defense: "Everyone else is teaching their kids." He wasn't going to have me be at risk. He wanted me to be a lady by day, but a killer by night if needed. We were training in the lake and around the property all weekend. "Erin, don't you roll your eyes at me." Dad was mad.

"Dad, I'm going to have to deal with high school boys, not angry militants."

"The skills you learn now with me will carry you forever. I have seen things no man should have to. I'm going to make sure you're prepared for anything. Hate me now, but you'll appreciate it when you need it." Dad was getting worked up.

"Okay, Dad, I love spending time with you regardless. If this is what you want to do for the holiday weekend, I guess I'm in. I'm not going to be happy about it, but I'm here."

"I think you'll have more fun than you realize." That was usually the case.

The first skill we worked on was dealing with your hands tied behind your back. He said it was to teach me to stay calm in high-stress situations, to control my breathing. I learned basic focusing techniques, breathing techniques, and multiple ways to get out of that situation. The one my father couldn't stand was the way I would loop my arms under my legs and get them in front. He thought it was cheating to get my hands in the front so I could work on whatever makeshift handcuffs he put on me.

"Erin, being flexible at fourteen doesn't mean you'll be flexible at twenty-five or thirty. There are no rules that say no one can harm you in your thirties."

"I agree, Dad, but I can stay flexible. Work on it, take yoga or Pilates."

"Always a smart-ass, just like your dad. Well, I guess we'll just have to practice both ways. If I put you on a chair, you can't cheat." Good point.

This went on for the whole weekend. We would keep coming back to these exercises. He worked with me on finding my way home without a compass or a phone, dropping me off in the woods a mile up the street and leaving me alone. You probably think this guy is crazy, but he was worried about me, wanted me prepared. Maybe he knew I was going to be a wild child living life as a spy.

"Honey, you may be asking yourself, 'Why is my dad doing this to me? He knows that I'm only fourteen, doesn't he?'"

"Not quite like that! But it's close enough." I smiled.

"Well, my only response is that I'm sorry I waited so long to get you started on this stuff. I'm going to push you more than your brothers. You need to be better, faster, and smarter than they are. If a guy is going to attack you, chances are he will be stronger. You just have to be quicker and sharper with your mind. Do you understand? It's about more than just being fast and smart." He always pushed it past the norm.

"Yes. I'll rarely be able to overpower a guy, but I can outsmart and outmaneuver him. I got it, Dad, I'm just glad we're hanging together. Plus, this shit is fun."

"I'm glad you think me teaching you life-saving techniques is fun." He smiled wide.

"I know my brothers aren't as into this stuff as much as I am. It's a bit crazy, but that's half the fun. Does Mom know we're doing this?"

"No. As far as your mom knows, we're fishing and camping out here."

"Got it."

I CAME TO from hitting the water hard, just as my father had taught me years earlier. I maneuvered my legs through my arms to get them to the front so I could untie myself. They hadn't used handcuffs or zip ties. Luckily for me, they used good, old-fashioned rope. With some teeth and wiggling, plus a few trips below the surface to concentrate, I was able to untie the ropes and begin my swim to shore.

By now, from the strong current, I had drifted well back from the boat, further downstream than I could have imagined. I began the couple-hundred-yard swim back to shore. Luckily, this area of the river is filled with sandbars and other obstacles; it's treacherous for boats, but great for tired ladies recently thrown overboard.

After I'm finally back to shore, people are looking at me funny. To break the tension of a group sitting on a blanket in the park I just swam up to, I started joking around.

"That was one bad date on the riverboat. I had to get out of there. Can I borrow someone's cell to call a ride to pick me up?" I laughed.

"Sure, I've got you, girl. That must have been some brutal date." She smiled back at me.

"You have no idea. First of all, he was supposed to be twenty-six, and I'm pretty sure he was forty."

After some small talk with the two girls sitting on the blanket with the two guys, they decided they would drive me home. The problem is that I don't have my keys. I don't have my phone or my wallet. They're all back in my car across town, but it's okay; I have a spare key in one of those magnetic boxes behind one of the wheels.

When you have a tendency to get kidnapped or involved in situations that can cause you to be gone for days at a time, you learn where to park your car, store your items, and have backups. There's a long-term parking lot at the edge of town, not near the house I'm renting, mainly to minimize people tracking me. When you get involved with drug dealers, international arms dealers, and all the nation's top criminals, you have to look over your shoulder continually.

I had the girls drop me off a block away in front of a house. I walked into the back through an open gate. I am always paying attention to who can see what I'm doing and connect the dots. I quickly sprinted through the backyard, hopped the fence, and made my way back to my car. Finally starting to dry off, I opened the glove box to grab my phone and call my handler to check in.

"Hey, meet you at Café du Monde in an hour to go over everything?"

"See you there."

Other than not being in prison, I think my favorite part of what I do is the cloak and dagger bit. I truly enjoy finding new ways to keep people off my trail, staying off the grid, and operating in the shadows. It's fun, knowing things and being aware of events that many will never know about or read about because of the work we do to protect them.

I made it back to my place, off Frenchman Street, a bit in the rough area. It's not the worst, but it's easier to hide when you stay in a place most people wouldn't want to visit. I found a place for rent from some slumlord scumbag, furnished it quickly with secondhand shit from all over, and now I have an off-the-grid place in New Orleans. I paid him upfront in cash for five years—well, my friends and me at the CIA. He doesn't know where the money came from, probably thinks I'm a drug dealer.

There are some cool features, like the high-end security system, along with a few hidden cameras and motion sensors around the property to help me feel safe for the few moments I get to sleep. As I jumped into the shower, with the hot water rushing over me, I started talking to myself. I do this a lot; I can have full conversations with my shadow. It helps me work through the complexities of the cases I'm on.

At this moment, I'm going through the key decisions that got me to this point. The life Erin used to lead, the one Marie now leads, and the choices in between. Some of you may know a colleague of mine, Neil Baggio. Because of me, there is a criminal out on the streets and Baggio's girlfriend is dead.

I know you're asking yourself how he can be my friend with all that shit going on. It's partly because he knows I feel horrible about Maria, but also because of what was happening at the time. My handler pulled him aside, spoke to him at her funeral, and explained to them what I got myself into and how Agent Garcia ended up the way she did. They had the whole thing on security footage from the gallery in Santa Fe.

Ms. Choike was in town, secretly with El Jefe, Susie Gaines, and one other cartel leader. Susie and her psychopathic brother Jason used their family's money and influence to create an enormous crime syndicate with plausible deniability to flood the nation with drugs. Ms. Choike's family tree is filled with criminals stretching all the way back to Poland.

While they were having their meeting, which I was in on, Maria tried getting footage to speed up the case, which she wasn't supposed to do. She was unaware of the access to the security footage we had already. When one of the goons for Gaines found her, they tied her up and began to torture her pretty bad. They began pumping her full of

Requiem to get her hooked and ruin her life. She looked like a shell of herself after only a few days. I couldn't take it anymore; I had seen what that drug in high volumes could do to a person. There was no coming back for Maria. I put her out of her misery.

I know what you're thinking: *Damn, that's cold-hearted.* If you were there, if you knew what I did and saw what I did, you would know that was mercy. Because of that, I will work tirelessly to make amends for her death, save as many lives as I can. We all have a purpose, even if it's to be a lazy piece of shit; the world needs all kinds. It's my job to make the tough decisions, to be cold at times, and to stick my nose where most people don't like it.

As for the witness, Bryan, from Gaines Chemical, I wasn't trying to kill him. I was merely trying to make it look like an attempt and use it as a way to get Jason Gaines's attention. What I was not aware of was the car I stole to crash into their caravan was loaded with gasoline in the trunk. That, mixed with the fiberglass frame of the Fiero, led to it ending tragically.

Those two deaths are on me forever, and because of them, I have sworn not to kill ever again. It's going to be hard, especially in the world I operate in, but it's a choice I've made, to try to rectify my mistakes. I've burned many bridges, and I know it may take a lifetime to fix them, but I'm willing to work tirelessly to solve them.

It's time for me, though, to head over to Café du Monde to meet up with my contact and be introduced to my partner for this case. I threw on some jeans—good and tight ones, because they're the only ones that don't snag on windows and fences when you're doing the things I do—a New Orleans Saints tee, a zip-up hoodie, and a matching Saints hat. I grabbed my backpack with all my on-the-road gear and headed out.

They have brought someone in freelance, outside of the normal chain of command, to help me. They know this case is sensitive, and it's going to take a unique set of skills. As I made my way down the street, I noticed a brutal pain starting to form in my jaw. I reached into my bag and grabbed a pain pill—nothing crazy, just a T-3. Essentially an over-the-counter pain med mixed with codeine.

I needed something to take the edge off and keep me moving. As I walked up to the café, I noticed my contact sitting in the back with two coffees and some beignets. He knows I don't want a coffee or that shit. He can be an ass sometimes.

"Phil, what the hell, you know I want water, not a coffee." That's not his name, just what I call him. He reminds me of Uncle Phil from *The Fresh Prince of Bel-Air.*

"Marie, shut up and drink your coffee. After the night you had, you should be lying down. I left you alone on that boat for three minutes, and you go and get tied up then thrown overboard?"

"Hey, you were supposed to have my back and tell me what might be coming."

"I'm here to observe, report, and get you intel. I'm not your sidekick; that's what they made me bring in, though."

"What? Another babysitter? Who'd I tick off now?" This is never-ending. Then again, I'm not in prison. Calm down, Marie.

"This person is going to be a go-between for you and me. That way, I can sit back and focus on gathering intel, and you two can operate in the field. We asked around for more than a week and couldn't find anyone, but your old boss found someone willing to help."

"Who, and from what agency?"

"He's not from a government agency, though he is former military. His name is Christian, and he works with Neil Baggio and Ken Chamberlain."

"Shit, there is no way. Not after the crap I pulled."

"They are fully aware of the situation. Your boss read them in on everything. Once they saw what happened, they wanted to help in any way they could."

We call any of our supervisors at government agencies "boss." It's a general term, since we never really know who we're reporting to. It's easier to keep it vague and move on. I've only seen Christian one time, but he was aiming a rifle near me, so I took off quick. It was the night at Gaines's tower when he was covering Maria and Neil. It was my job to be on the lookout for people. I saw them and let them go. I wasn't about to stop someone from a rescue.

"You're telling me that Neil saw the video of Agent Garcia and me? I'm so screwed. Hell, Christian is probably here to shoot me."

"No, he's not. I'm also not aware of everything that was shown or said to Baggio. Christian specializes in the kind of support you need. After the show you put on today, you need more than what I can offer. He'll be down here first thing tomorrow. You can ask him yourself how Neil is doing. You know what it's like working with BCI; they're turning into their own spy agency."

"I know. The cases they keep taking on have them growing more than anyone expected. And they keep filling that void no agency wants to touch."

"That's the point of getting them involved. We need someone to work with you that can't be tied back to any agencies. Remember, the deal is you don't go to prison, but you're still kind of a free agent."

"I know. I get to work and stay free, but if I get caught, there is no government agency coming to rescue me." I know, a great deal, right?

"Hey, the other choice is a federal prison for ten to fifteen years."

"I know. Do you have contact info for Christian?"

"I just texted it to you. I'd touch base with him tonight so you can get organized for tomorrow."

"I will. Other than giving me shit and telling me that you're not going to be helping me in the field, what else you got for me?"

"It turns out the guys that tried to kill you over the money you stole are linked to a local drug dealer who controls most of the action in New Orleans. His name is Andy the Brat."

"He legit goes by that name, or people call him that?"

"That's for you to figure out."

For the remainder of the meeting, Phil persisted in giving me shit. He followed up with some intel to get me started on tracking down Andy. He likes to hang out at a place called Café Negril on Frenchman Street. It should be easy enough since I live close and love live music. So sitting around and trying to find him, not horrible.

"I guess I'll talk to you on the phone or texting. No more in-person visits?"

"Exactly. I'm actually heading out of town for a bit. I'll be on the other side of Lake Pontchartrain."

"Okay, I'll make sure and call you if Christian kills me."

"Shut up. You know he won't."

Walking out of Café du Monde, I headed back toward my place. To be safe, I took the long route and worked my way toward Bourbon Street. With my hat pulled down, hoodie, and backpack, I could pass for a street punk, which is the look I'm going for; people don't like to look someone in the eyes they think is homeless or struggling. It makes them feel bad. I know that avoidance can make people feel a bit inhuman, but it works.

I shot Christian a text message, asking him to call me when he gets a moment. I wanted to go over the case, feel him out, and get organized for tomorrow. I wouldn't mind finding someone to have fun with tonight either. Hey, I'm an attractive woman, twenty-nine years old, and I still have the same body I did in college. I mean, there are some scars and wounds that didn't used to exist, but I still like feeling good about myself. As for the twenty-nine part, it's a funny story. No one knows how old I am. I like to keep it that way. I'm great at lying, as well as looking the part.

I could have hung out with Richard Grieco and the 21 *Jump Street* crew. I've been able to pull off looking as young as nineteen, and as old as forty. I'll let you decide how old you think I am based on pop culture references. Hey, Grieco had looks that could kill; it made me turn on some Color Me Badd, that's for sure. I also had an older brother, and my closest female companion growing up was my aunt, who was about ten years older than I was. If that doesn't give you a hint of how old I am, I can't help you. You're going to have to get used to being in the dark with me, it comes with the spy territory. It's always a guessing game.

See what I did there? I gave you references to an age, then mixed it up and gave you plausible reasons to ignore your instincts. This is how I am so good at my job; it's also why my government would rather use me as a loose asset than throw me in prison. I was almost back to Café Negril on Frenchman Street when my phone went off. I had my earbuds in, but I'm assuming it's Christian. I don't feel like taking my phone out of my pocket.

"Hey, what can I do for you?"

"Erin, it's Christian. Sorry, I mean Maria. It'll take me a minute on that one."

"You're fine, Christian." No, he is. He's hot.

"I was just following up like your text asked me

to, about tomorrow and the next couple of days."

"Yeah, I'm going to start trying to find a drug dealer, a leader in the area, tonight. I'll text you the info, where I'm starting, his name, etc. That way, if something happens, you have a starting point."

"I appreciate that; you know how we are at BCI. Details, details, and more details."

"I know. Speaking of which, how is Neil doing? I know I screwed that one up. I felt I was doing what was right, but I understand why he and others might hate me."

"He filled me in on what was shared with him. He and Ken saw the video, and Neil said if someone hadn't told him it was Maria in that video, he wouldn't have believed it. He said that, though he's still upset, he can understand the decision that was made." Ken is Neil's longtime friend and business partner in their private investigation firm, BCI.

"If it's any consolation, I've given up that aspect of my life. And for the record, I never intended to kill Gaines's head of security, just make an attempt on his life. That shit blew up in my face, literally and figuratively." No joke.

"Well, rest assured Neil wouldn't send me to help if he didn't think you were worth helping. If he had even a bit of an issue with everything, he would have told the powers that be he couldn't do it."

"I know. It makes me want to do as much as I can to help him moving forward. I know Susie is behind bars, but we still have lots to do with Jason."

"We'll get there; we always do. As for the current case, what's up?"

"We're trying to track down a pretty big player in the drug business down here. He goes by the name Andy the Brat."

"These drug dealers and overall street entrepreneurs love their fun names. They're not nearly as cool as the old mob ones, though. We have a guy up here called Brock the Butcher. He's trying to change it to Brock the Boxer."

"Isn't Butcher better? At least it makes people fear you."

"Not if you got the nickname because you accidentally shot up a meatpacking warehouse."

"Okay, that shit's kind of funny. Back on track, though, this guy is tied to a bigger name with Gaines. I just don't know who. I have intel that said he was supposed to do a big deal with a different gang. I stole their money, so they couldn't do the deal, to buy me some time."

"How'd they take that? The money-stealing part, that is."

"Oh, they threw me off a riverboat while tied to

a chair."

"So they took it as good as can be expected. What do you need from me?"

"Well, Christian, there is only one way to say this. I need someone to watch my back and make sure I don't end up dead before I can figure this shit out. I tend to get in some messy situations."

"I bet that's why you're great at your job. It's that fearless nature that gets you in there. Sometimes it's that same drive that can put you in a shit spot. I got your back; I'm assuming you want a wide perimeter to operate?" Christian gets it.

"Exactly. We can communicate with earpieces on ops, or phones and text otherwise. I'll keep you up to date on what's going on and where I am. If I don't think it's going to be dangerous, then you can investigate, and we can work on it from two sides."

"Good. For a moment there I thought you were going to have me just watch from afar nonstop."

"I've already got enough people at BCI mad at me. I'm not about to tick you off too. I'll see you tomorrow. Hit me up when you land. Are you going to need a lift?"

"No, I've got a car to use when I get down there. Ken has a friend that's going to leave me an old truck to use so I blend in. It's an old work truck that belongs to a military buddy of his."

"Does Ken have a friend everywhere? I've

heard stories of his connections."

"From what I can tell, almost. I'll see you tomorrow, Marie. See, I got it this time."

"Thanks, Christian."

3

"I've been here for two months . . . no idea."

I was standing outside on the phone for quite some time, trying to muffle my conversation, but there wasn't much I could do. After I got off the phone with Christian, I walked into Café Negril. It's as if someone took a small coffee shop that had a stage and built a half-ass bar and makeshift kitchen. I love the feel of the place. The stage is small; it looks like your back porch was stolen and dropped inside, ten feet from the bar stools.

The music tonight is some rock-type blues group. They have the usual suspects: A singer, drummer, and two guitarists. I'm pretty sure one of them is a bass player, but don't quote me on that. I'm not a music major. The sound is supposed to remind me of Clapton, B.B. King, and Van Halen, if what I'm reading off the flyer the door guy handed me is true. I listened to Clapton with my dad as a kid.

Enough playtime. I need to get some info. I guess I'm going to have to take off my hat and play flirtatious girl with the cute bartender. I have practiced, sadly. I know the best way to pull off my hat and flip my hair. I've had some boring stakeouts; you do things to pass the time. I know a large part of my ability to get intel and sneak into places relates to my use of the power of female sexuality. I'd be lying if I told you the power I have over men three times my size isn't invigorating.

The bartender was a young guy, probably twenty-two, with boyish cute dimples and thick, dark hair that goes past his ears. He fits this bar perfectly; I bet he kills with the tourist ladies. He's not very tall, but neither am I, so that's not a big deal.

"Hey bartender, what's your name? I'm Marie. I'm new in town, looking for some fun places to hang out. Anywhere else I should check out?"

"My name is Charlie. How long are you in town?"

"I'm not sure yet; it's for work. I'll probably be here a month, at least. I never really know. It just depends on where the work takes me."

"If you're going to be here a while, I say stay

here for the night. I'll tell you what other places you should go to in the morning over breakfast." Shit, he's fast and smooth.

"Aren't you cute? We'll see how you play your cards tonight; those dimples will only get you so far."

We went back and forth, flirting for a bit when I brought up needing a smoke. We went back and forth about cigarettes. Eventually he realized I was asking where I could score a joint. I mean, there are murals of Bob Marley on the wall, and it's a pretty obvious vibe in here. Plus in the world I have operated in lately, being around hardcore drugs is part of the deal. So weed is like asking someone for a glass of water at this point; it shouldn't surprise anyone.

"I have a little bit, but if you're looking for the dealer around here, it's the guy over there." He pointed at the cook.

"Do I need to order my to-go burger different to get some weed?"

"Very funny. No, just go over there and talk to him. If you're just looking for a simple one-hitter, we can go out back and take a hit."

"Let me talk to your boy for a minute. Then I'll be back."

I made my way over to the man behind the grill. He was not your stereotypical dealer. I mean, he looked like one from TV, but it's my experience that little white boys deal drugs more than anyone else. I mean, TV and the news might tell you otherwise, but anyone who needs something other than the legal shit will tell you it's always some little white guy named Pooky or something.

"Hey man, how's it going back there?"

"You mean other than hot as hell and humid to match it?"

"Yeah, that's what I mean. Your buddy over at the bar said you're the guy to know in here."

At that moment he looked over at the bartender, they exchanged smiles, and then he smiled at me. He walked away for a few minutes, which seemed odd. While I stood there waiting, I noticed he was burning a burger on the grill. As he came back, I noticed he had on a fanny pack.

"All right. What are you looking for tonight? Something to bring you up, or something to chill you out?"

"Nice fanny pack. I'm just looking for some weed and information. I'll pay for both. I just didn't want to put you in a position, so I'll buy the weed too."

"You're not a cop, are you? Everyone hates the fanny pack until they want what's in the fanny pack."

"Good point, and no, I'm not a cop. I'm

something different. I'm an insurance investigator trying to track down a missing painting. I have some intel that tells me your boss, Andy the Brat, might know something that could help me. I'm trying to protect an investment. I don't care about the law." It sounds plausible, for making it up as I go.

"Well, that's a mouthful; it's a good thing you're sexy as hell. And cash always speaks loudest. How much are we talking?"

"Here you go, this should cover one costly bag of weed." I handed him three B-Franks.

"That will do. As for Andy, I can get you in touch. I'm not gonna have to hunt you down for the money after I get you the info am I? Is this work or pleasure? Andy will want to know, and so will his gate keeper."

"I'll pay you up front. Make it easy. I'll even take all the risk. And it's a bit of both, I mean look at me, I fit in your pocket and I come with a smile. I'm harmless." I smiled and did my best impersonation of a commercial sales girl.

"Leave your info with Charlie over there. I'll get ahold of you later tonight or tomorrow with some info. Sound good?" He turned his focus back to the grill.

"It'll have to be, right? How about that weed?"

"Oh, you were serious. Here you go." It'll help

him stay focused and think I'm worth the work.

"Hell yeah, I need to take the edge off." I haven't smoked since college.

"Enjoy. Charlie is a good guy. I mean, he's a bit of a slut, but he's a gentleman slut."

"Thanks for the intel, on both fronts."

"Want a burger?" He smiled.

"No, you burned that shit to a crisp."

"Fair point." He laughed and tossed one in the garbage.

That guy was a stitch. I didn't even get his name. I guess I can ask Charlie. He was a big dude, too, about six-foot-four and easily two hundred and fifty pounds. He was built like an ex-NFL player or something; I hope I don't end up in his crosshairs.

"Did you get what you needed over there, Marie?"

"Huh, yeah. Your boy took care of me. What's his name?"

"No idea; we call him LT, on account he looks like a left tackle. I seriously don't know his name. I've been here for two months . . . no idea."

"He also said you're a good guy to know. He said you're a bit of a slut, though."

"Oh shit, he threw me under the bus on that one. I can tell no lies; I enjoy working in New Orleans behind a bar."

"It's okay. I don't mind that." I said, smiling back at him.

"Does this mean you might hang out until the end of my shift?"

"I'll tell you what. Why don't we go on your break, enjoy that one-hitter, and see where the night goes from there. I could use a bit of some fun after a long week."

"Give me five minutes. I'll meet you out back. There's the door over by the bathrooms. That's where we go to take smoke breaks."

"I see it. I'll go to the bathroom and meet you over there."

He met me out back to take a hit off the weed that LT just gave me. It was easy to get him riled up, especially armed with this blonde hair and LT's tidbit that he's an easy bartender just looking for fun. If I make them think the bar is low, they won't think I'm a threat. The whole point of getting them to think I'm nothing more than a cute groupie trying to get in touch with Andy is to lower the threat level. That's the plus to having the frame and hips I do. Sadly, most men, even the good ones, can be easily swayed with a little love and attention. I know my looks can be used as a weapon. Shit, any spy knows that. It comes with the territory. It's more about disarming people than anything else. It's not about the sexuality of it all.

I need to get my mind out of the gutter. If I stay around here, I might end up going home with Charlie, and that's not a good idea. I'm only human. Even if I'm trying to use him, I still have urges, mixed with a few chemical enhancements. It's time to make a smart decision. I can't have him involved like that. I need him wanting to impress me to get with me. That motivation is the best way to get someone to vouch for you. I walked right out the front door and waved to LT, giving him the call me sign.

I'm hoping our boy Charlie finds the number that I put in his pants pocket. I gave him one of the dummy numbers that I use with Google Voice on my phone. It's nice having three different numbers on one phone. However, it can be a bit confusing every once in a while.

The bouncer stopped me on the way out to give me a bit of advice. She also scared the shit out of me. She was small, but had way more tattoos than I do. I know what you're thinking: *Marie has tattoos?* I do. I also use that temporary tattoo company Inkbox to mix it up. It's great because I can put them on, they become part of me, but fool some of the people when I take them off. It's kind of like Clark Kent's glasses and Superman.

"Hey miss, what are you doing?" She said with

a judgmental smile.

"You mean, besides heading home to get some rest?" I was trying to duck down and ignore her.

"You can't leave without my number. My name's Chantal. I think you're sexy as hell."

"Thanks. *You're* quite attractive yourself." I sound like a teen boy; then again, I always fumble when girls hit on me.

"Well, don't be a stranger. I overheard you saying you might be in town for a while. I'd love to show you around town."

"Thanks for the offer. I might just take you up on that."

On the way back to my place, I did a few cut-throughs, running through yards, just in case someone was watching me. I didn't want them to know where I lived. I couldn't shake Chantal from my mind; she was attractive, though she could probably kick my ass. I might enjoy it; she had that dangerous but soft thing going for her.

I'd like to tell you I'm straight, gay, or bisexual. I'll be honest: I don't even know anymore. I lie so much for a living, fake it with guys so much, I don't know what's real anymore. I do know I'm lucky enough to have supportive parents. When I was in high school, I had a close female friend that my parents assumed I was dating. We might as well have been, but neither of us could admit to the other how we felt.

I remember when my mom pulled me aside and told me that you can't always choose whom you love. There is no right or wrong way. As long as you're not harming someone intentionally, just live your best life and live honestly.

Finally back to the place I'm renting, I threw my bag on the floor, kicked off my shoes, took off my pants, and plopped on the couch. Oh shit, I wanted to grab a beer before I sat down. It's so far away. Maybe I have superpowers . . . nope, that didn't work. I guess I'm stuck here, no beer, and no energy to make it off of the couch. Good thing my phone is charged and there's a blanket nearby.

4

"Not all of us can have a memory as prodigious as Neil's."

W aking to the sun coming into the condo is always pleasant, that and the chill in the air from the beginning of spring. The weather out here in March isn't too bad: cool at night, warm and wet during the day. The nights are pretty nice, but not nearly as nice as the weather in Santa Fe. Oh, I miss that shit. Even on days when it would get up into the eighties, you could count on the nights dropping to fifty or sixty.

As I grabbed my phone, I had to laugh. I already had a few messages from Charlie and Christian. Charlie was being a cute puppy, damn near begging me in a polite kind of way. As for Christian, he messaged me when he boarded in

Detroit, letting me know he'd be here around nine in the morning.

Since it was only eight, I still had a little bit of time to get ready. My morning regimen consists of three things: Flintstones vitamins, a prenatal combo vitamin, and a pre-workout supplement that gives me a kick. Uncle Phil had also sent me some more intel on the group from the boat. He was able to pull even more connections to Andy, as well as some crews working locally, allowing me an easy in.

This job isn't all action, as everyone likes to think it is. I'd say the majority of my work as a spy is researching and preparing intel for when it's needed. It's about having the right tools and leverage for when the time arises. I can't always be in the great action sequences. It would be fun—exhausting, but fun. The truth is that it's a ton of waiting for guys like LT to get back to me, flirting with guys like Charlie to build trust and finding a way to gain access to Andy's inner circle.

Of course, getting into the circle is the easy part. It's picking the right entry point that can be tricky. If you gain access to a crime syndicate, but you do it with an underboss that has no pull with the top brass, you're screwed. That's what all the downtime is for: Researching, scouting, and digging into everything. It may not be pretty, but it's the truth.

Fresh and clean, I'm rocking a V-neck, some tight jeans, and my favorite tennis shoes—bright red Pumas—along with a Georgia Bulldogs hat. In New Orleans, I like sporting a tee and a hat pulled down. It allows me to keep that cute, younger girl look while still going unnoticed. When you are constantly in and out of places, being forgettable is the best way to go.

As I was making my way over to my car, parked back in the long-term lot, I realized it's going to cost me more than a hundred bucks to leave the lot when I could have just taken a cab or rideshare. I have a 2010 Jeep Wrangler Renegade, with a crap-ton of miles on it, and all the sides and top off. I got a great deal on it because there isn't a top for it, which probably isn't the best thing for a town like New Orleans. But I did get a half cover at a body shop to minimize some water to the face if it does rain. It's a standard, which I love, mainly because even open, no one touches it because they can't drive it.

Having an old manual like this can be a little bit of a pain, but overall, it has its advantages. I know it's a bit of a cliché to have a cute girl in a Jeep driving around New Orleans, but it works. Christian texted me a few minutes ago, letting me know he had landed and that he will get ahold of me when he gets his car. I told him to touch base with me when he got settled, and we could meet up for muffuletta at the Central Grocery in the quarter.

I was back at the apartment when Christian texted me, saying he was heading toward lunch. I wasn't in the mood to keep driving, so I just jogged a bit from the house toward the deli. It's only a few blocks from my place. As I was walking up Decatur Street, I could make him out from a block away. He still looks great; he's fit, a smidge under six feet, with blond hair and blue eyes. He's wearing a T-shirt tighter than the jeans I'm wearing; maybe he stole it off a little kid. I'm not complaining, though, just pointing it out.

"Hey Marie, how are you doing?"

"Just enjoying New Orleans, getting thrown off boats and such. You know the life we lead; there's never a dull day."

"I'm glad to hear that you're okay. You know you have a nasty bruise forming on your chin? You did a good job with the makeup, but this isn't my first rodeo. You get punched pretty good?"

"Yeah, right before I was thrown off a boat. Kind of regretting telling a guy he wasn't strong enough to do it."

"I'm assuming he was?"

"Sort of; the edge of the chair I was tied to didn't

clear the bottom deck all the way, so he got me over the ledge on the second level, but he didn't have enough in him to get me and the chair to clear the boat. Which was good, because it freed my hands from behind the chair."

"There is a lot to unpack there. How about over lunch you walk me through in more detail what info you have on the case and where we need to be?"

"Sounds perfect."

Christian and I were lucky enough to find a spot inside. We split a full muffuletta. Well, I had about a quarter; he ate the rest. He claims it was from not eating all day, but the food is so good here I just think it was the fresh olive salad.

We spent the next hour going over all of the moving pieces down here. I explained to him about the money I stole, what it was being used for, and what we needed to do with the guys, the ones related to that circus freak who threw me off the boat. I'm assuming they thought they killed me, especially with how he ended it and how far the current pulled me away from the boat. By the time I came up, I was a good two hundred yards away. There is no way they would have seen me, which means, as of right now, I'm a ghost to them.

They were just low-level's working for Andy the Brat. They were looking to use that cash to score a large quantity of the street drug Requiem, something that Christian and I have plenty of knowledge about.

"Let me see if I have the gist of this. Andy the Brat is trying to buy large quantities of Requiem to start distribution in New Orleans. The money you stole was for a deal he was conducting, which delayed them on this purchase."

"Yep, it's a shit-show kind of week down here. Between the humidity and having a drug syndicate after me, this should be fun. That's why I need the backup. It's more than likely going to get messy."

"Well, what's your to-do list in all of this? Where are we starting?"

"We're already doing it. See that younger guy behind the counter? The one next to the older couple that looks like they've worked here for decades?"

"Yeah. What about him?"

"He's their nephew; he's also a glorified screw-up. According to Uncle Phil, he's a runner for Andy."

"Who's Uncle Phil?"

"He's my handler, for lack of a better term, as a free agent in the wind. He looks like Uncle Phil from Fresh Prince. He looks after me too, like an uncle."

"Uncle Phil, I got it. What do you need from me,

then, like right now?"

"I want you to sit on him, see if you can follow him back to where Andy is, or where his base of operations is."

"I can do that, but it'll be hard to keep an eye on you too."

"We might run into each other; I'm trying to set up a meeting with Andy."

"Let me get this straight. You stole money from him, and you're trying to get his attention more than you already have?"

"Now you got it. This is my style, up close and personal. I'm going home to change into something less obvious. I'm supposed to have a contact get ahold of me about a meet. Technically I stole money from people close to Andy. There's a good chance he doesn't know it was me."

"And if he does know it's you? How will you handle it then?"

"Some charm, and when that doesn't work, a little violence."

"Funny, you and Neil would be best friends in another life."

"I hope he can forgive me someday, even if he has to punch me; it's an option I'm willing to offer. Just throwing it out there."

"I'll let him know."

I walked out, leaving Christian to his task, and

headed back to the house. I am surprised I haven't heard from LT; then again, if they partied hard, he might still be sleeping. I shouldn't be too surprised that a guy involved in the drug game isn't an early riser.

My day was filled with checklists, errands and to-dos. I had a haircut— much needed, both for personal grooming and for safety. Those riverboat guys are looking for a specific lady. A few of my temp tattoos came off today, which also helped. That plus a few wigs I picked up will keep me quietly moving in and out of where I need to be without too many people asking questions.

Meeting Christian went well, and now I'm going to have someone officially watching over me. He's done some fantastic things in the military, as well as BCI. The reputation he has built over the past couple of years is starting to precede him everywhere he goes. He's kind of the quiet type, and he doesn't even realize he's hot as hell; that's the best part. He's always business, all the time. It doesn't hurt when the guy you work with is a hunk. The other guy is more of the Cheetos behind a desk and wipe it on his pants kind of buddy.

While getting ready, I realized the hairdresser took off way more than I had anticipated, but I told them I was going to be wearing wigs, so they knew what to do. It's barely past my ears, not quite a bob but not quite a pixie look either. I mean, I still look cute as shit, especially with a hat on; I just can't do the big, flowing hair trick unless I'm in a wig for a while.

I guess I'm going to have to learn some new tricks. Good thing I've got an abundant supply of V-neck shirts. That look, tight jeans, and a bright push-up bra will allow me to manipulate the male species. I'd say to coerce men, but these aren't men. Christian is a man; he knows how to treat someone with respect. These other creatures I will be dealing with are barely functioning humans. The goons in the underworld aren't known for their deep conversations on the economy. Though I say that, I have come across a few of them over the years whose grandmothers and mothers have taught them manners. There is always hope.

Around four o'clock, just as I was losing faith, I got a text from LT, telling me to call when I had a minute. A woman has to play hard to get in all these situations, so I took my time and worked on a light blond wig with bright blue highlights. With the tattoo sleeve on my right arm, highlighted with blue, this should hit just right. After a good fifteen minutes, I called LT back. I hope it's good news.

"Hey girl, it's LT, from the bar last night." Even he says "LT."

"Hey man, it's Marie. What's up? Any luck with

landing me a meeting?"

"Sort of, I was able to get you a meeting with one of his lieutenants. Diego is his name. He's kind of a hard-ass, but he's a pretty good dude."

"Good dude for your line of work, or good dude in general?"

"Oh, he'll kill you, but he's respectable about it. I think he went to Tulane and even graduated; you'll see what I'm talking about when you meet him. He's too smart to be a street punk."

"Well then, how or where do I meet Diego?"

"There's an Irish pub he likes to play pool out of. We can find him over there. He said to show up there within the hour. Can you meet me there? I'll text you the address; it's off Burgundy."

"Got it. I'm meeting Diego, an intellectual Latino drug dealer, at an Irish pub in the French Quarter. Nothing sounds messed up with that at all. Does he know I want to meet Andy?"

He chuckled.

"Yes, he does. Keep that attitude, and Diego will eat it up. That'll get you to Andy. Diego is the gatekeeper to the boss."

"Sounds good." See? A day of what felt like uselessness gets me where I need to be.

Off the phone, I finished getting ready, changed into an emerald green V-neck and some cute green Chuck Taylors. Hey, if you're going to play the role of the cute and somewhat naive girl, you need to put effort into selling the point. Not all of us can go through life like Neil, always wearing his favorite Detroit hat, T-shirt, and jeans. Oh shit, I need to order some stuff and look for an Amazon pickup point to at least improve my closet. Am I becoming the female version of Neil? Shit. I mean, I do live out of a duffel bag; maybe it's just our uniform.

By "our" I mean all of us vagabond investigator types that get fixated on cases and forget to shower. Except for Neil; that man showers more in a week than a family of six girls. It's hard not to be impressed with him, his carefree attitude, and his no-nonsense approach to cases. He gets shit done, works his ass off, and rewards his team. He's damn near the perfect leader, and I killed his girlfriend. Son of a bitch, I keep slipping into that thought process.

I pulled up my phone to check the notes I had on LT, Charlie, and this Diego guy. Not all of us can have a memory as prodigious as Neil's. Most of us have to use different tools to stay on top of shit. The plus side is that I can think fast on my feet.

I can read a room and make the right decision in an instant. I wasn't always that way; my dad, as usual with the strengths in my life, had a way of forcing me to learn. He would put me in the hardest situations possible and force me to study at the same time. Walking into a room with a crew and their leader is always one that requires fast thinking. Lately, it's involved me committing murder or aiding in it. These are the reasons I have promised myself I'm done with that part of the job, at least for a while. I'm not sure I can come back from another dark run like that. If LT is right and Diego can help me get to Andy, I better not mess this up.

5

"Got it, boss. My bad on bringing her here."

Y ou can call it foresight or paranoia. Either way, I made it this far because of the foundation my father gave me. The summers made me who I am. My mother would tell you it's just in my DNA. I'd have to agree a little bit, but training a young teen like a future spy for their safety probably played a role. At the time, I just thought my dad was overprotective, but as I grew up, I realized he was preparing me for a life of adventure and risk. I think my favorite story is from when we had been training for a few weeks. It was the weekend before July 4th.

"Erin, you need to listen up. When we started these exercises, it would take you nearly a minute to get the answers correct. Now you are able to do them in thirty seconds or less. This means you're getting better at managing stress and functioning mentally under duress."

"I get that you want me to do better in school, but how is asking me questions while I tread water in a weight vest going to help me?"

"Everything in life is about practice. If you think you will do well in a situation you've never prepared for, you are relying on luck. Preparation and practice, and yes, these crazy exercises, get you ready for the unknown."

"See previous question." I was a bit sassy.

"Exhaustion, physical duress, and mental challenges teach you that you can operate and survive anything. The more you are in these types of situations, the less likely you will get worked up when something happens." That was a good point.

"Okay, Dad, I'm going to trust you. I always do. What's the next set of questions?"

We spent the next hour doing this exercise, pushing me to exhaustion while having me recite small poems. We were practicing science that I struggled with last year as he explained to me why it was necessary. He kept me going, kept pushing, but was building something inside of me that would be impossible to break.

Dad had a really good point, explaining how during sports championships, you will often hear people speak of being there before. Having experience in high-pressure situations matters. It allows us to slow down and not get worked up. Where others may be stressed out or mentally challenged, those with experience and practice can function at a higher efficiency. It's the experience gained and preparation put in that allows champions in any sport to succeed.

"Erin, you may think I'm crazy, but this will save your life someday. I have a feeling you are going to be more adventurous than me."

"I know, Dad. I enjoy it. It's not like I hate it. Maybe that's a sign of things to come."

"Maybe you can follow in your old man's shoes and serve your country in your own way."

"Like a spy, I can see myself getting into the CIA! Especially if you keep training me like this."

"You better keep your grades up and study some different languages if you are serious about it."

That's the day I decided I was going to do more than just embrace the time with my father and push toward the goal of an agent. I knew I was going to have to learn a few languages. I picked Spanish and French because they're similar to each other. Being Latin-based would allow me to learn different languages with similar foundations. I had some foundation already in Spanish; my mother taught us the basics as kids, which made it an easy language to pick up in high school.

From there, I began studying French and bits of Italian on my own. I started looking at languages as ways into different parts of the world, different cultures. With that knowledge, I could travel the world and truly experience it. The summers with my dad became a ritual until graduating college. He would work with me on things, push me, and challenge me in every way possible. In the summer of my junior year I let him know what my goals were in life. He suggested that I not tell Mom until I'm ready. Not the worst idea, since she's the worrywart of the family.

Finally pulling up to the pub, I noticed how small it was. I shook off nostalgia mode. I had to get my mind right, get focused on the situation in front of me. This guy is the only thing stopping me from getting to Andy, which will help me stop this whole operation. I guess I'll find out if they recognize me and think I'm the woman who stole all their money.

The bar is what one might expect for an Irish pub in the French Quarter. Fahy's isn't big, but it's not too small either. It fits in perfectly downtown, with a few pool tables, a big U-shaped counter, and some old parents tending bar. They looked like a married couple running their bar into their forties and maybe fifties. As I walked in, I noticed there was a small group of Latino men, a little overdressed for the occasion, and one guy who it looked like they were all keeping an eye on. I took a shot and walked up.

I know you are asking yourself, *Where was LT? Why didn't you wait for him?* Well, the biggest reason I didn't is that I work better without a chaperone.

The bar was mixed with a little bit of everything and all different ages. It was your normal New Orleans hangout.

"Hey, you must be Diego. I'm Marie. LT told me to wait for him, but I'm a bit impatient."

"You're lucky you're not a big guy, or I'd have one of my boys teach you some respect."

"Are you saying that it helps that there's an attractive girl standing in front of you?"

Right then, some guy walks out from the bathroom. He finishes drying his hands with the paper towel he's holding as he approaches me. He points to his guy to get up from the seat. Now I see why they were all looking at him. He was sitting in the boss's chair while he was gone.

"I'm Diego, that's my idiot nephew Miguel. He's a good kid, just needs to learn some respect."

"I didn't mean to cause any issues; I was just coming to meet you. I apologize for not waiting for

LT to walk me in, but I got a little impatient."

"It's understandable. Marie, did you say? LT is usually late; I wouldn't be surprised if he shows up twenty minutes from now."

We both laugh a bit and start to talk more freely. It's small talk, stuff you would ask someone you were flirting with. I know he's into me; he's also used to being in power, so I have to pick my times to push. Right now isn't one of them. Almost on the dot, twenty minutes after we were supposed to meet Diego, LT finally walks in. Damn, Diego was spot on.

"Mr. LT, twenty minutes late as usual. Good to see you're consistent."

"Sorry boss, I got caught up doing a run. Figured you wouldn't want me to turn down the score. Also we have another problem with Tito and Dennis. You know, from the boat issue the other night?" Shit, is he talking about me?

"Hey LT, we don't talk business in front of the lady. I know you said she bought from you, but still, that's personal." He chuckles and puts his arm around LT.

The two of them turned away for a few moments and started talking. I could only make out a few words here and there. They were definitely talking about the issue from the riverboat the other night. I could make out something about missing money and a girl. I could feel the hair on the back of my neck stand up. I had to slow my breathing and make sure I stayed as calm as a summer breeze. The last thing I can do is let off the vibe I have anything to do with that situation.

"Now, what are we going to do about this lovely young lady?" Diego smiles at me, like nothing happened.

"I vote for buying her a drink for starters and getting to see if she can play some pool." LT's breaking the ice.

"Sounds like a plan. Can you shoot some pool, Marie?"

"Only if we play 9-ball. I'm not a fan of the other ones." I could feel my stomach turning.

"Well, we are gracious to our guests, so I'm up for some 9-Ball. LT, rack 'em."

So here we are hanging out in an Irish pub on the edge of the French Quarter playing pool. I have to watch myself because I'm kind of a pool shark. I played a ton when I went to school. Going to college at Georgetown and being a cute girl allowed me into social circles I might have otherwise struggled to break into. There were plenty of pool tables in the frat houses, private clubs, and mansions where I often found myself impressing a group of men. I might have been smarter than them, but they were more impressed with my talent on the felt.

As we played a few games, we went back and forth about school and growing up in the south. He's originally from Baton Rouge, but his family moved there from Texas. I tell him I'm from Alabama. It's close enough to Georgia in both geography and lifestyle, so I tend to tell people that's where I grew up as an easy cover. He asks me a few questions about Andy and why I want to meet him. He doesn't beat around the bush very much. Every so often, Diego would dip to take a call, answer a text or talk to LT. I kept piecing together that they had found one of the men from the other night, dead. It sounds like the guy that threw me off the boat started killing his own men, thinking they helped me take the money. With each call, text or conversation, my heart jumped a bit, and I felt a little sick. It's not that I don't experience fear. It's that I've learned to ignore it and move past it.

"So, Diego, what can I do to get you to trust me more so I can meet the boss?" It's not so subtle, I know.

"Aren't you forward? Let's finish this game, and I'll think of something. I still don't understand your reasons."

"Well, I feel like we're doing this dance, so I

figured I'd speed up the tempo a bit."

"Fair point. How about we play a game, no holding back. If you beat me, I'll set up a meet, and If I beat you, I wan–"

I cut him off. "How about if I lose, I give you five hundred cash and a rematch tomorrow, for double or nothing." I won't need it.

"You're on, but to make it interesting, let's do a few shots of tequila first, then relax for a minute to let it settle in."

"I like your style, Diego. Let's do some Casamigos if they have it."

"As far as you're concerned, they only have one brand, and it's going to burn. You're not going to back out, are you?"

"No, but can we get it chilled?"

The last thing I want is for him to see me as a threat or a badass. However, I can drink most liquor neat, which is my preference. It has a tendency to upset some people, especially of the male persuasion. I learned quickly, especially in college, that the male ego is frail. What many of them won't tell you is that they are scared shitless all the time around women. The only ones that aren't are sociopaths and sexual predators.

As we sit there dropping back shots of tequila, I remember one significant fact about my ability to play pool. Most of the time in college, I was pretty drunk when I played, which means my inner Black Widow comes out when I get trashed. No, not the Avenger. For those of you who a bit lost, Jeanette Lee is and has been one of the top pool players in the world. I know it's a high bar to set, but we all dream of being Kobe or Michael on the basketball court at some point, so you get it.

"Well, Marie, let's do this. One game of 9-ball to see if you get to meet Andy?"

"Sounds good. Who gets to break?"

Some of you might be saying to yourself, *Marie, this is too easy*. Like I said before, it's not hard getting into these gangs at the lower levels. They are used to high turnover and giving people small things to do. It's about building trust little by little. They feel like they're in control all of the time and that at any moment, they can simply end you and break ties. That's the reality of it. Getting in is the easy part because gangs have a problem with people getting arrested and dying. Sad, but true. The inner circle at the top might be tight-knit, but these aren't global organizations like Gaines Chemical. The corporations that hide behind lawyers and boards are the real criminals. These groups are nothing comparatively.

A petite girl that would pop in every once in a while, whisper in his ear, and then leave. I rarely got a look at her, as she would almost come out of the shadows and then disappear. After the second time it happened, I heard one of the guys say something about Pan. That must be her name. Diego has people filling different roles all over. I can tell from my interactions with the guys at Café Negril and my short time here.

While playing pool, there were a few times Diego asked why I wanted to meet Andy. He pushed on a few occasions, doing his job. When I made him feel confident enough, I was just some girl looking to meet the boss. He lowered his guard a bit. He'd seen plenty of motivated women before, and I know how to play the part. There's also the chance that Diego doesn't like his boss and has no problem putting the snake in the room with him.

"I'll let you break since this is my table and my home felt." He was feeling cocky.

"Sounds great. By the way, when's the last time you got cleared off the table without picking up your stick?"

"Oh, look who's talking shit!"

As I took turns flirting with him and sinking balls into the pockets, I couldn't help but laugh. It's just like I had imagined it, but the shots are even crisper. If this were a movie, it would be a montage of shots hitting pockets at an alarming rate. I move through each ball as if I'm cutting warm butter. As I line up one last shot, he finally begins to speak up.

"It's safe to say I just got hustled pretty hard. Don't miss this last easy shot."

"I'll tell you what. I'll make this last shot with my eyes closed. If it goes in, not only do you have to introduce me to Andy, but you'll owe me one: A big one. Or you can give me a grand! Your choice of how you want to pay it off."

"Deal." Before he can even finish the word, I close my eyes and drop the shot.

"Game, set, match." I know that's tennis.

"Son of a bitch. I guess I completely got played. Well, let me get your number, and I'll set up a meet with Andy. As for you, LT, you're in this shit too. We both owe her a favor. I don't care how big it is. We may be hustlers and thieves, but we have honor, especially when we get schooled this bad."

LT hangs his head. "Got it, boss. My bad on bringing her here."

"Don't be. There's nothing sexier than a pretty woman who can hustle you out of your pants and your bank account on the felt." Diego's smiling.

It's one thing to have a father who pushes you to do better, but you may be asking how can you be great at so many things. Well, the answer to that is that my social life was all about preparation and making the right moves. What I mean is that at Georgetown, I spent most of my time working the angles, practicing things my father taught me. I worked on counterintelligence techniques, read up on the human condition. I told you that at a young age, I decided I wanted to be a spy, an agent working cases. I took it seriously; it also helped my father push me to the edge and sometimes over. We had plenty of fights over the years, especially when I decided to go away to school in D.C. He was upset I was going so far, but he understood.

I think his biggest concern was that he couldn't have as big an impact on my life with me that far from home. He wasn't going to move the family farm and uproot my brothers and mother. They were staying local, the two oldest boys going to the University of Georgia. My youngest brother went to Georgia Tech on a full academic ride. The kid is brilliant.

But back to besting Diego. He was saying something, but I was kind of ignoring him.

"Thank you for the compliments, Diego. Unless we're going to relax and hang out, I think it's time for me to head out. It's already getting late, and I have an early day tomorrow. That is, unless I can meet Andy tonight?"

"I doubt we can make that work, but I'll make the call for you."

"I need to call a friend and check in. Do you mind if I step outside? It's girl stuff."

"No problem. Talk to you shortly."

Don't get me wrong; being a woman in my line of work can suck. I am frequently looked at like a piece of meat. I take pride in my looks and the overall package I present, but I wish I weren't looked at like a fancy car. I'm not an object, though I have to play one in many scenarios. It's the world of espionage, the way I get to most of these shallow-minded men. I can't believe that line of "girl stuff" always works. I need to check in with Christian, since the night could take a turn. I want to give him a heads up that I might need some backup.

The night is going better than expected, since I seem to have Diego's attention. He is willing to stick his neck out for me with Andy. Batting these lashes at him and snaking him in pool has built up a false sense of trust. The phone rings a few times, no answer. I guess I'll just text Christian.

While I'm waiting on him to call me back, I start thinking about what I might say to Andy. I was snapped back to reality by my ringing phone. Christian, finally. Though it felt like more time had passed, it hadn't even been ten minutes.

"Hey Marie, sorry for the delay. I was tailing someone, following up on a lead. But I'm good now. What's up?"

"I'm downtown at a bar called Fahy's. It's an Irish pub. I can text you the address. I'm trying to meet with Andy tonight. If we do, I'll text you the details. I could use some cover or backup just in case." I don't know why I didn't tell Christian that they might recognize me. I guess I'm still new to this partner shit.

"I can do that for you. I'll make sure all my gear is good to go and head to that area so I can be close if something goes down."

"Thanks, Christian, we can follow up later if needed. Do you have any new intel, or just working on it?" I need to speak up.

"Just working on it. I'll let you know if it becomes something we can use."

"Sounds good. Thank you for the support down here. Hey, before I forget, there might be a chance that the guys from the boat the other night recognized me. It looks like the main guy is killing off his own men, trying to find a lead on the cash."

"You really think that means he's connecting the dots? Or are you just worried? Do you need me down there quicker? Just say the word." Christian was getting worked up, as expected.

"No, I'm good. I'm just letting you know what's going on. I'm not used to sharing in the middle of a mission. Sorry, I'll get better."

"No problem, we all want the same thing: Gaines to eat shit and end up back in prison."

"Fair point."

"I need to get back in there and keep up appearances. I'll text you if anything changes. Thanks again."

"That's what I'm here for, Marie."

As I walked back in, I saw Diego was still on the phone. This makes me feel a little better, since I thought I was out there for an awfully long time. Then again, I think quickly. Even my memories go fast. They may be detailed, but they move quickly. LT was in the corner, sipping on a beer, and waved me over.

"It looks good. I think he's getting Andy to swing by and meet you." Or kill me. Maybe this is all a setup. I could feel my heart pumping. I knew it was just my mind racing, but I couldn't help it.

"Thanks, LT, I appreciate it. Also, I hope I didn't get you in trouble for hustling your boss."

"Nah, girl, he loved it." LT smiled. "He likes it when people take charge."

"Well, that's good. Want to mess around and shoot some pool while we're waiting?"

"I think we should wait for him to get off the phone. The last thing I want to do is be loud and distracting to him."

"I see. Well this is your backyard; I'll follow your lead."

We sat there in an uncomfortable silence, just listening to the music in the background. While we waited for Diego to get off the phone, I began wandering around the bar, looking at the different things on the wall, the knickknacks and such. I found myself working my way around it until I was ordering a drink, trying to calm my nerves. For a moment, as I dropped off my empty glass at the bar, I saw my hand shake. Something I rarely, if ever, see. That shit from Santa Fe still has me spooked.

"What can I get for you, miss?" I love southern respect.

"I'll take a glass of tequila, neat, whichever top shelf you have."

"Single or double?"

"Three fingers?"

"You're in New Orleans. You *know* that's acceptable." The bartender gave me some shit.

"Then three fingers it is."

As I was getting my glass and pulling some cash out, I heard someone behind me. It was Diego. He wasn't about to let a lady pay for a drink when he's around. Well, that's what I hoped was going to happen.

"I'll take one, just the same. She's buying, though." Damn—well played, Diego.

"Yeah, it's the least I can do. Would you like salt to rub on that wounded ego?"

"Damn girl, that hurts a bit. I guess you don't

want to hear what Andy said."

"You win this round. Barkeep, I'll pay for it." I handed her cash.

"Let's sit back over there by the pool table. We'll have a little bit of time to kill while we wait for Andy."

"You lead and I'll follow." As I try not to quiver in front of you.

Back in our corner at the pool table, LT racked them up and we began to play. This time it was a bit more fun, not as serious. I got to know Diego a little more. He majored in business management and marketing at Tulane and even completed his master's. He intends to go back to that world, but he makes too much money doing this gig with Andy. Diego is the man in charge of making Andy's businesses look legit on paper to keep the feds and others off his back.

It also allows him to live a lifestyle out in the open. The best part of it all is that many people don't even know who he is. That's where the name Andy the Brat comes in; it's just there to give Diego's boss cover.

I texted Christian a message in a code I came up with on the fly. Since I was going to be dealing with Diego and some other guys, I saved Christian's name as Christina in my phone. That way I can text updates without looking obvious. I pulled out my phone and texted him to let him know the meeting was going down there. I hope he understands it.

"Hey girl, I'm staying at Fahy's maybe until close. I might get to meet a good friend."

I got back a simple message, "Gotcha," from Christian. It's a good thing too, since as soon as I texted him, Diego became interested. He leaned over my shoulder and started to look at my phone.

"Calm down, Diego. I was just texting my friend, letting her know what I'm doing. We do that to be safe if we go out alone. Would you like me to show you?" I flashed my phone at him.

"No, we're good. I'm just a bit nosy. It's an old habit. I like to protect Andy from prying eyes. That reminds me, I need you to sign something really quick before you meet him."

"You need me to sign something? What are you going to have me sign an NDA or something?" LT walked up and put a tablet in front of me.

"You're beautiful, great at pool, and smart. How many guys have asked you to sign an NDA?" he said, joking.

"At least one other one." At Georgetown, it was as if every frat boy had one ready to go.

"All right. Well, let's get it over with. I can have them email you a copy."

"It's okay. I'm a fast reader, but I'll have you email my cloud drive so I can save it."

"Won't even give us your email. I can appreciate being safe."

I quickly read over the document; it was only two pages and was straightforward. I decided what the hell, the name is fake anyway, so I have nothing to lose. Come to think of it, I don't sign Perdita ever. This is going to be fun. I signed it "Marie P" and a squiggly line. You know, all fancy-like.

"Now that we have that over with, when do I meet Andy?"

"He's standing right behind you. Marie, meet Councilman Kevin Andrew Schwartz."

There he stood, like something out of a Welcome to New Orleans guide. Slick hair, second only in shimmer to his shoes. He took his suit jacket off to look casual, but still looked the part just the same.

"So that's where the Andy comes from, and now I get the brat part. You grew up a little rich kid. I'm sure your friends called you a brat. . . . Sorry for the 'tude, it's a habit. It's a pleasure to meet you."

"You were right, Diego, she's a looker and smart to boot. Not everyone knows who I am. You did your research. Did you have an idea it might be me?"

"You know the rumors are out there, but no one

will confirm it. I guess I know why that's a pretty good NDA you have there."

"Not sure we'd ever use it in court, since it would mean I'm already in jail. It's more for scaring and keeping people quiet."

Diego spoke up. "Boss, why'd you tell her that?"

"She's too smart to think otherwise. It's okay. I don't think she's going to tell anyone. She wanted to meet me for some reason. A little birdie told me you want to get to Jason Gaines and his drug ring." He's fishing, but doing a good job of it. I'll play along.

"That's true. His drugs killed my sister." You know, the one that doesn't exist.

"I'm always up for a bit of revenge, as long as it makes good business sense. I'll tell ya what. I'll help you if you can find a way to keep it from hurting me financially."

"How am I supposed to do that? I don't even know your system."

"Then you'll just have to hang around more, do some work for us, and get to know the operation. Then find me a way to help you and keep the money flowing."

"I can appreciate a pragmatic businessman. Sounds like a plan."

For the next couple of hours, we just sat there

talking and drinking until the bar was closing down. I eventually had to excuse myself from the night because I wanted to get home in one piece. I called a ride share service to pick me up.

"Hey guys, it has been a blast. Andy—I mean Kevin—nice to meet you. I'm assuming you can just have Diego or LT reach out to me. I'll make myself readily available to you for the next week or so. Don't hesitate to call me in the morning."

"Sounds good, Marie. It was a pleasure meeting you. I look forward to our plans."

As my ride showed up, I jumped in and got out of there quickly. I know my car might get a ticket, but I'm not going to risk getting a DUI, not after the shit month I've had. As I sat in the car, my head spinning, I noticed a text message from Christian, saying he saw I made it out. He asked if I knew who Andy was. I texted back, "Councilman Kevin Schwartz."

6

"Son of a bitch, we need to find out what's going on with the local case."

I t's six in the morning and I hear a pounding at the door; well, I assume it's at the door. It might be my head from all that tequila I drank last night. It's not typically my drink of choice. I prefer vodka or a light beer. I know it's girly, but it's essential to watch what I put in my body, especially with the crazy schedule I keep.

There it is again; it's definitely someone at the door, not my head. No one has my address. Who the hell can it be? I get up, grab my pistol, and put it behind my back as I walk to the door. As I look out the peephole, my heart and head pounding in unison, I see it's just Christian. I sigh and open the door.

"Dude, how the hell did you find me?"

"Who do you think called me down here? It was Uncle Phil, as you call him. I asked him where you were so I could wake you up. We have a busy day today. Get ready. I'll go run and grab coffee and breakfast from down the street."

"Let me get ready. With short hair, and the fact I'm not Neil, it'll only take me a few minutes."

"I guess I'll just sit here on the couch and watch the news on my phone, seeing as you don't seem to have a TV."

"Christian, your sarcasm is noted. I'll be out in a minute."

It only takes about fifteen minutes for a quick shower. It's just about cleaning off and getting that humid stank off me. I may have walked out in only a towel to give him an update on me getting ready. I'd like to say that I'm not sure why I did it, but I know I did it to get a rise out of Christian and to make him keep his eye on the prize. I think he's cute, and I'm flirting a bit.

"Hey Christian, I'm almost done, just need five more minutes."

He turns, eyes wide, and almost stutters. "No problem. I'll just be here."

"See you in five."

I walk back in and "accidentally" leave the door cracked. He can't see anything, but the anticipation has to kill him. It's how I am by nature; I like to have control. Too often, I thrust myself into situations where I need to flow with it and make shit choices for survival. It's nice when I can manage things on my own terms. I step back out of the bathroom and get his attention.

"Hey, Christian, let's get going. Where are we off to for breakfast?"

"I have no idea. I just got into town. I know you've probably been there a few times, but can we get Café du Monde?" He looked so serious.

"Sure, I'll stop with you, but we'll get it to go so I can hit the French market to get something better for me."

"Fair enough."

We make our way out the door, both looking over our shoulders. I tell him to go out the front while I go around back and meet him at the corner. Some habits are hard to break, and with a case like this, I'm going to work as hard as I can to keep a low profile.

"Did you see anyone following you? I cut through a few neighbors' yards before I came back out."

"Marie, do you really think these guys are already onto you?" I'm always in that state of paranoia, even if I'm calm.

"I'm not sure, but I can't be too careful.

Especially after excavating the funds they were planning on using for Requiem."

"Speaking of that, what is the total amount that was taken? Just wondering."

"A little over five-hundred grand. Why, need a loan or something?" I smiled.

"No, when I was watching the news, I saw a story of an investigation into a half million-dollar heist from the city fund." Was he always going to be this serious?

"Wait, what the shit?" How did I miss that?

"It makes sense, since Andy's really Councilman Schwartz. Son of a bitch, we need to find out what's going on with the local case. I'm going to call Uncle Phil; you reach out to Ken, and let's see what we can dig up. If I have money from the city, we need to find a way to get it back to them."

"Yes, all in due time ... but what happens if the councilman just takes the city funds again to bankroll his operation?"

"You've got a point."

While we continue to walk to the café, we both make our calls. After a good minute, I start to back off of Christian, just to leave some distance, so we don't look like we're together. I know it's partially paranoia, but in this business, that shit keeps you alive.

Phil says he thinks the same as Christian; we need to time it right. He is concerned we could be handing them the money back to do with what they please.

I think if we find a way to get it back there without a trace, there will be too much heat for them to try again. We can also keep an alert on the accounts with BCI's government contacts to ensure it doesn't happen. The other question is, did Schwartz use this as an opportunity to clear his name, since he doesn't have the funds? He has to cover his tracks, since I have the money he was going to use, then put back. Without it, he needs to answer for it, under his day job as councilman.

"OK, I just got off the phone with Ken. He said he's going to run a few ideas by Neil and TJ and see what they come up with. For now, they want us to sit on the money. They don't want it to end up being traced back to any of you or to us. They especially don't want it being used to purchase a massive quantity of Requiem."

I'll always accept help from TJ, a tech genius who heads up BCI's computer intel division.

"Thanks, Christian. As for the news, were there any other stories that caught your eye this morning?"

"There was one about a missing girl tied to another council member's family. She's seventeen and has been gone for a week now. You don't think there's any connection, do you?"

"Not sure right now, but how about you do some digging while I work on Andy, Schwartz, whatever he's going by? To ensure I don't slip up with him, let's just keep calling him Andy for now."

"Works for me. Let's head over to the market and grab something for you. I have my donuts."

"Those are beignets; don't let any local hear you call them that."

We walk down the street from Café du Monde to the French market. I love what they've done with the place. I have traveled to New Orleans many times, for work, and for fun in college. The market has changed over the years. They added a new roof, larger fans to keep it cool in the heat and overall gave it a new feel. That has allowed more small shops and food vendors to come in that are amazing. You can always find a great chef getting started, with fantastic food and presentation.

With food in hand and a few new pieces of jewelry, Christian and I head our separate ways. He's going to work with a contact Ken and Mike, from the Detroit FBI office, had set up for him to aid in the search for the missing girl. I'm heading into the city to track down Andy and his crew. The truth about cases like these is that they take forever to warm up, but once they're running they don't stop speeding up until the grand finale.

For instance, I'm just waiting around Jackson Square looking at art and hoping to get a call soon from LT or one of Diego's associates. It seems like the afternoon is going to be shot; on a lark, I message LT to see if I can speed this along and he replies, "Sleeping, I'll hit you up after four."

I guess I have some time to kill, so let's go do some shopping. Not the kind you're used to, the type that involves me getting ahold of Uncle Phil to set up a weapons buy. While walking through the square, I'm approached by an artist, someone whose work struck me.

"Is there anything you like, madame?" he says with a French accent.

"I know New Orleans has a strong French heritage, but you're not from around here, are you, sir?"

"No madame, I am from Quebec, actually, just outside of Montreal. I came down here to paint, and for the warmer weather," he says, smiling.

"I do love this painting; it grabs my eye whenever I come through town. I just don't have the place to put it. I travel too much for work. What's it called?"

"I call this piece *Fille Perdue*."

The painting was the silhouette of a young

woman looking out over the city from atop the Westin. The skyline is breathtaking. Something about the colors and the way the girl is alone speaks to me. There is no light around her, just darkness and shadows, with the light and energy of the city below her, just waiting for her to engage. It's not surprising it speaks to me, as I'm walking this world more alone as each day passes.

"Lost Girl, huh? No wonder I like it. I need to get going, but I'm sure I'll see you again."

"Have a great day, madame."

With my mind distracted by that painting and those words, it was time to get moving. I am going to need to increase my firepower and possibly obtain a Taser. I don't know how often I can shoot legs and limbs to keep this no-killing vow going strong. Uncle Phil was able to hook me up with a contact, which was good because it's not like I can walk into Walmart and get all the things I need. With this kind of heat on me, Andy's goons are looking for the money, and now Christian and I are digging around this mess. I need to be prepared. I'm used to acting surgically, without so much as a small arsenal. I bet you anything this missing girl is a way for Andy, or Councilman Schwartz, to deflect the missing money to someone else. I can see a pile of bodies ending up on the news and some press conference claiming the girl is saved, and they were also the robbers. That's how this world works. It doesn't have to be plausible in court. Sometimes it just has to be enough to change the news cycle.

There are always contacts the CIA has for people like me or Christian to get what we need in a town like New Orleans. I picked up two different Glocks: One with sight, the G17 Gen5, and a Glock G26 Gen5, for those hard-to-conceal moments. Just to be safe, I had them throw in a modified AR-15 to allow for quicker, longer bursts. Some knives, ammo galore, and a care package of things I might need, such as explosives, finished the shopping spree.

While they packed it up, organized it, and received payment from Phil, I went back to the house and grabbed my car to pick everything up. It's not like I can be walking that much stuff over to my place. I probably should put some of this in storage. This means pulling the electrical schematics online, renting a place, and pulling some wires to the unit for an outlet or two to create a small backup hub. I just need enough to power a laptop, charge a phone, and run a 5G hotspot. You'll be amazed by what you can accomplish with some wire cutters and an outlet from Home Depot. I currently have six places across the country for just such an occasion.

After a few hours, I dropped off some ammo and a gun at the storage place, then made my way back to the apartment to get ready and wait for LT's call. It was going to be another long night, I can assume. I decided to use the time wisely and ride the exercise bike while researching the councilman and the missing girl on my tablet. I spent an hour researching and riding, getting my heart rate up.

The more I read into it, the more I'm certain the councilman looks connected to the missing girl case. It looks like the missing girl's father is eyeing a run at mayor on a platform of cleaning up the streets. His big push is drug rehab and being hard on dealers. That might be an issue for someone looking to move freely in the city and push a new drug into which they are about to invest millions.

While Christian is investigating the missing girl, I'm going to spend my time on Andy, as well as the current mayor, to see what I can come up with. I'll also have to look into the police chief since there's always the chance that they're the primary contact or cover Andy has. I can't be short-sighted about what's in front of me. It's almost five when I decide to head to the shower that I finally see that LT messaged me. It's an address with a time: 6:15 p.m., somewhere outside of town. I guess I'm going to have to get ready quickly and get driving.

I'm going to shoot Christian a call in the meantime.

"Hey bud, how's it going? I finally got the message from LT."

"Where you headed?"

"Out to the other side of Lake Pontchartrain. I have to be there a little after six, so we'll see if I make it there in time. I'm packed and good to go. I'll message you if it gets hairy. Any news on the little girl?"

"I was able to get TJ and Ken to scan the info that the locals have and send it over. Then Neil's buddy at the FBI hooked me up with a local contact to see if I can help. That way, they won't give me shit if I'm around." Christian always spoke calmly.

"That's great. Do you think there's a chance Andy is tied to it all?" I was looking for confirmation.

"It doesn't look like the authorities have a direct connection. Not sure they're even looking at him. But it makes sense. He's tied to drugs. At least that's what we know now, and the girl's father is anti-drug."

"Aren't most of us anti-drug? That aside, it's hard to look into Schwartz if you don't have the connection we do, knowing he's Andy the Brat," I said while getting on the freeway.

"Good point. Do you have any new info on him?" he asked.

"Yeah, I think it's got his fingerprints all over it. There are too many connections and blindspots in cases that involve Andy and the police are nowhere to be found. We need to look into the police chief and the mayor. One of them is giving him the cover he needs to pull this shit off."

"I already have TJ and our FBI contacts seeing what they can pull on them. See if there are some investigations of rumors that might help us. I'll keep you in the loop. If something changes and you need me out there, just holler." Neil's got his guys trained tight.

"I'll send you the address when I get off here. I should come up with a message to keep it less conspicuous if I do message you."

"Just text me the phrase 'Can you grab a bottle of wine?' I'll know what it means."

"Easy enough. I'm about to lose signal. I'll message you as soon as I get there so you know when to be on alert." Like that, I was back on my own.

Off the phone and on the bridge, I'm realizing this thing gives me the willies. I don't know what it is. It might be that it's a little more than twenty-three miles across a body of water.

As I approach the end of the bridge, I see that my GPS is telling me I should turn off soon. This might be on the water somewhere. It looks like I'm driving into the St. Tammany Wildlife Refuge; at least that's what the signs say. What are we doing out here? I hope they're not going to kill me; that would suck. Before I pull up at what looks like a trailer converted to an old house some decades ago, I text Christian. I want to make sure he can find my body later. I joke, but it keeps me from being too scared in these situations. Speaking of jokes, there's LT, smiling at me as I pulled up, shaking his head.

"Hey Marie, glad you found it okay. It's kind of tucked back here in the middle of nowhere."

"You can say that, but what are we doing out here?" I was back to playing it cool.

"Think of it as a little initiation and seeing what you're capable of." Oh great. Thanks, LT.

"I'm both intrigued and scared." Mostly scared. I'm losing my edge.

"No need to be scared; the boss just wants to speed things up. He has some stuff going on." LT was trying to be cool.

Yeah, no shit, he has some stuff going on. He's stealing money from the city, using it to buy drugs, and he's trying to be a drug kingpin like his buddy Jason Gaines. I still have no clue how they're connected. It's not like Gaines can simply call up all the politicians and ask if they want to buy drugs.

"I take it we're going inside?" I say as he leads me to a door.

"Yeah. Follow me and be quiet. Don't talk unless someone directly asks you something."

"Okay, I got it. I'm the new girl."

As we make our way into the trailer, there is a Barbie doll in the mud by the door. I'm sure I'm reading into things, trying to connect Andy to the missing girl, but I can't stop my mind. LT opens the door, and I step in to see some guys and a girl standing around a small table with a map on it. The place is a dump, something you would expect to see as the scene of a crime. I know it's humid out here and dirty, but it's disgusting. As I shake the shit look off my face, I hear one of the guys speak up about the job at hand.

He's a tall guy, dark chocolate skin, and stands over six feet. He's good-looking for someone older. I assume he's in his fifties, but he's in great shape, and that silver hair is a good look for him. I hear one guy talk to him and say his name was Sage; it's fitting for a wise-looking gentleman.

"Hey Sage, get to the point, man. I know you're the veteran of the group, but we're going to fall asleep at this rate." The guy standing next to Sage is the one speaking.

"Man, shut up. All in due time; we have a guest today. You can call her Marie, no need for last names around here." Maybe it's actually his name, not a nickname.

"Hey, everyone."

"What do we need another girl in the crew for? We have Coral." She's rocking puka shells. These have to be nicknames.

"It's okay to have another girl around. I can only deal with you guys so much." Thanks, I think.

"Andy wants her to work with us on this job. He said she'd come in handy. He's pretty sure she'll be a good fit. His crew, his rules!" LT says.

"Understood, LT!" they all said in unison.

Altogether there are five people in this trailer, including myself and LT. We have Sage, Coral, and one other guy. He looks squirrely as shit. My guess is they call him Squirrel. I'm going to enjoy seeing where this goes. Come on, Squirrel!

"You obviously know LT, you've met Sage, and I was introduced. That just leaves…." Coral was cut off.

"Guys, let's get back to it." So close! What's his name?

"Sage is right; let's get back to business. We have a job tonight to pull off. It's not going to be easy."

"Wait, aren't most of our jobs easy? That's the point of having Andy lead the crew," Coral chimes in.

Sage finally got control of the group, but still didn't introduce the crazy dude. As you've seen, I'm playing a game in my head as they go through their names. You may ask yourself what I am doing. It's a thing I do to keep myself busy when I'm supposed to be quiet. Otherwise I start running off at the mouth.

Back to Sage and his words of wisdom. He's going over plans for a heist of some sort; it doesn't sound too complicated or difficult. The crew's going to hit a secret stash of money and drugs that were moved off-site from an evidence warehouse.

From the sounds of it, Andy found a way to get it moved to a location that would be easier for his crew to steal it. I'll have to figure out how or why he's not suspected of anything with these brash, risky moves. He seems like an arrogant prick that is used to getting away with murder. Maybe he's just that dim; he did bring me into his crew, and I stole the half a million from him. He's a great judge of character, if you ask me. OK, back to the plan.

We're driving up to the storage facility that will have the loot Andy is going to use to replenish his stolen money. I'll give him this: Instead of focusing on the lost money, he just worked on a new way to fund it. At least he's got some ambition and his eyes on the prize.

We know exactly which unit to hit, but the goal

is to make it look random, so they need the extra hands to cut some locks and make it look like we're searching for something. That way, they can say it wasn't targeted.

The only way they can be confident in this plan is if they have help in the police force somewhere, controlling the message and investigation. Otherwise, it doesn't make sense. It doesn't work out.

We're riding over in a van and an older truck. I can't help but think I'm in a bad heist movie, especially when they started tossing out masks. That's when I showed my true colors. You don't think this girl was going to trust her hair and face to some random ski mask some dudes had, do you? I always come prepared, and on our way out to the van, I grabbed one from my car. It's just a workout face mask, but that mixed with my sunglasses and a hoodie covers me up well enough.

"All right everyone, time to get ready. We're about to pull up; remember your assignments. Rabbit, you and Marie go in first, get the door open, then start your search. We'll do the rest and circle back here."

Right then, I notice Sage give Rabbit a look. I'll be honest, I might just be pissed that his name isn't Squirrel. I take my phone out for a quick second and text Christian the address, delete it fast, then text him the message about a bottle of wine. Something doesn't seem right. It just feels off.

"Hey, what are you doing over there, girl?"

"I just messaged my friend asking her to pick up some wine for later. After this, we're supposed to hang out, but I won't have time to grab one since I'm helping you guys."

"LT, look at her phone really quick."

LT comes over, looking at me like a pissed-off parent. He grabs the phone and scrolls through it. He even goes back to see if there were other messages. When he sees there isn't much else in the phone, except what he and his buddy had sent me, he gives me the look of death.

"Sage, it's just a message to some girl asking them to grab some wine."

"Okay, Marie, you're lucky. Let's get this done. If you don't mess this up, maybe we'll give you a code name. But you have to earn it."

Rabbit and I go up to the back door; he has a code and gets in with ease. From there, we go around with bolt cutters, cutting off locks, one after another, then we randomly go down a row opening storage units. We see some pretty cool things, some sad things, but nothing of consequence. When we find one with something valuable in it, we run to the truck and load it up.

PERDUE

The cash and drugs are going in the van. That way, they can stash the truck and take the van. This heist is about drugs, cash, and a ton of misdirection. Being on the inside, but knowing what I do, I can't believe these guys think no one would put this together. They also don't know they have a spy in their midst. This is going to be fun as long as I don't get caught or killed.

After fifteen minutes of opening storage containers and running out to the truck with Rabbit, I notice the van is gone. They obviously got what they were looking for. I look around, trying to gauge the situation and what's going on. That's when I feel someone slam me into a wall, nearly knocking me out. My head hit hard, forcing me to the ground. As I try to focus on where the truck is, I roll over and see Rabbit and Coral in the vehicle, driving off. LT, Sage, and the gang leave me here, either to take the fall or to see how I'd respond.

I don't have much time to figure out what to do or get my bearings. I lean into the wall, my head spinning a bit. With my back now pressed against the wall, my heart pounding and my mind racing, I am pissed. These assholes think they can just leave me here. They don't know I have a ride, but still. I have to focus, find some cover, then call Christian. In the meantime, I can text him.

CHARLES D'AMICO

What's your ETA?
Fifteen!

7

"I heard that about you. You're human, like the rest of us."

I guess I don't have a ton of time to kill, but I'm going to see how far I can get from here. The last thing I want to do is stay put. I can assume the cops are on their way to pick me up. I wouldn't be surprised if the crew called them, just to tidy up the bow. I send Christian another message telling him what direction I'm headed from the storage facility.

Luckily for me, it's not in the middle of nowhere. I'm able to get to a subdivision with houses and other cars where Christian is able to find me with an address I sent.

"Marie, you good?"

"I'm fine, just mad as shit. These guys don't know who they're messing with."

"Do you have any ideas? Want me to drive up the street the storage facility was on, see if any commotion is going on?"

"Yes, please do, then head towards the first address I sent you. I think I'm going to look for a car to steal. That way, I can pull back up and get my Jeep. But I'll have you stay close in case something else happens."

"I can do that. We're coming up on the storage place now."

As we drive by, we see a few police cars at the facility. They officers are talking to an employee. I wonder what they think is going on or if they're even aware of what was stolen yet. Someone will figure it out soon enough.

"Well, I guess it's good I have some backup and got out of there."

"That would be a hard one to squirm out of. Did you at least have your face covered?"

"I'm no rookie." I pull out my mask and shades, with a little chuckle. "Come on, man. I feel insulted."

As we get a little closer, we find an older-model truck, nice and easy to boost. With the windows down, all it takes is a quick hot-wire and I'm on my way. Christian goes ahead of me to park about a mile out so he'll be close if I need backup.

Pulling back up to the old trailer, I see only my Jeep and one other car. It's LT waiting for me, smiling. What does this jackass have to say?

"Damn, you made good time. I told them it wouldn't take you long to get back to your car."

"This isn't the first time I've had someone pull this shit. As a woman, you're used to being underestimated."

"I can see that, but I didn't know what you'd expect. You know all crews have their way of judging someone."

"I take it I passed, or is there another bullshit test you're going to throw my way? I've got better shit to do."

"Calm down. You're a good rabbit!"

"Wait, what? I thought that other guy's name is Rabbit?"

"No, his name is Squirrel. Sage just did that to mess with you." I knew it!

"Well, LT, Ms. Rabbit, at your service. When's the next gig?"

"I'll let you know. For now, take your cut, have a good night and enjoy your bottle of wine. Andy has something much bigger in store for someone as resourceful as you, especially being on the outside of our crew."

"What does that mean? It could still be the head

wound from your asshole Squirrel slamming me into that wall, or I might have just misheard you."

"Your bottle of wine, from the text earlier. The cash in your car and the real reason you were out here. It has to do with something Andy wants from you. He'll reach out eventually. I'm not sure when. He only tells me so much. "

"No, I meant my cut. What cut?"

"It's in your glove box. Have a good night." He paused for a moment, began walking to his car, then I saw someone get out of the passenger seat. It was . . .

"Andy, how's it going? To what do I owe the pleasure?" He loves this cloak and dagger shit, but he plays it off like a shitty B-list actor.

"You wanted in, and wanted to meet me. You've gone through a lot of work to get to this moment. What are you going to do with it?" He leaned into me, like a man with too much power often does to a lady like me.

"That's not what this is about, if you were wondering. I needed a new home, and your name kept coming up in some of the circles I was dropping in on. I don't like swimming with the little fish. I like to find the leader and introduce myself as fast as possible." He kept pressing on me. It took everything not to introduce my knee to his testicles.

"Well then, what can I do for you?" I could feel the hairs on my neck begin to stand at attention, like good little soldiers alerting the rest of my body to prepare.

"This is going to be a mutually beneficial relationship. Think of me as the thing you never knew you needed. I'm not sure how long I'll be here, but I'm sure I can be of service while I am. I like to come and go. Like a mystical vagabond." Now I sound like the shitty actor, but he's eating it up. I can see the wheels slowly turning.

"I'll think of something. We have a few projects that could use an . . . outside perspective. I'll reach out soon." He pushed back, smiled and walked away.

"Thanks again for a great evening." And the ringing headache, asshole.

Like that, LT and Andy walked to their car and drove off. Here I am, sitting in my car in the middle of nowhere in the pitch black. I reach into my glovebox to find five dollars. How cute! I text LT with five smiley faces. He just responds with a thumbs up, such a prick. This is the life I lead, and the choices I've made. I figure I'll call Christian and tell him we're good to head back towards the French Quarter.

The drive back is a bit annoying. I keep trying to think through the case, but I can't keep my thoughts straight. I want to check my notes on my phone, even add to them, but I can't; I'm driving over that damn bridge, and it's dark. I turn the radio up to some local jazz station. They say the song I'm listening to is John Coltrane. I'm not someone who can tell you the difference between Coltrane or Miles Davis. I'm getting the practice, though, being out here.

I managed to wind down a bit on the drive, quickly get changed in my apartment and run over to the bar. I end up beating Christian. I shoot him a text, and he lets me know he's five minutes out. He had to stop at his place to grab a few things.

Walking into the Three Muses, the first thing you notice is the vibe, from the aroma of the fantastic cooking to the live music filling the air. It's a joy for the senses mixed with food for the soul.

I approach the bar, ask the bartender for a menu, and sit down. I take out my phone and add details about the crew and their characteristic features to my notes. As I've said before, I can't power through this mentally like Neil; the stories I've heard about him are crazy. I need to be able to read it, to see it, and visualize it. If you've ever seen the *Sherlock* series on TV—not the British one, the American one—you would have seen them make one of those boards with all the notes and connections. I do that on my phone. I use a sales tool to keep it all organized; as someone who usually claims to be a pharmaceutical sales rep or just a sales rep for hire, it's an easy place to hide these things.

"Hey Marie, have you even ordered anything yet?" Christian surprised me.

"No, I sat down and began looking over some notes and making more."

"I heard that about you. You're human, like the rest of us."

"Yeah, that Neil shit is another level. I couldn't function that way."

"He always says it's just an ability to sift through information, not always remembering it by detail. But it's crazy, no matter how you explain it."

After a few rounds of small talk, the bartender comes back and gives me a bit of shit for disappearing into my phone, especially in such an amazing place as this and a town like New Orleans. I put my phone away and decide to simply enjoy the night, what little is left of it. Christian and I sit there talking about our pasts, getting to know each other and building some trust.

This night, a little bit of a buzz and the fact that he came to my rescue have me worked up a bit.

Hey, it's not only guys that can think about that stuff. It always cracks me up how in movies and TV it's some major event when a woman thinks about sex. It's like, come on people, it takes two people to make a baby; we think about it.

Shit. Now Christian is looking at me funny.

"What gives, Christian?"

"I asked if you've ever been here before, and you just looked glazed over."

"No, this is my first time. I usually hang out at the Blue Nile and Café Negril, but I just saw LT at Café Negril and don't want to run into him. If we do, we'll just say we're on a date."

"I'm okay with that. You'd be a huge step up from the girls I usually hang with."

"I doubt that, you're a good-looking dude. Don't sell yourself short." He acts coy.

"Seriously, I usually hang out with military or athletic girls, cause that's how I meet them. I don't think I've ever hung out or talked with someone like you."

"What about that cute girl I've seen around BCI? She's attractive."

"You mean my cousin? No thanks." He laughs.

"Okay, my bad. So how did you make your way to BCI?"

"Well, I'm a Marine, did a few tours overseas, and one of my COs on my last tour was friends with Ken. He introduced me, said I might be a great fit when I got back stateside. The rest is history. I worked up the food chain from low-level cases, cleaning the warehouse, a grunt. Now I'm a lead and working some of the higher-end ones."

We continue going back and forth, exchanging stories about getting started in our fields. Since he knows how I made it from the top of my field to burned spy, we skip that part. I keep turning the story back to him, and how he grew the reputation he has from his time with Neil and his team. Eventually, we get back on task, going over some notes and emails that Phil and TJ had sent each of us. Their findings only strengthened our hunches on Schwartz's ties to the missing money and girl.

It looks like there are lots of photos that connect the two councilmen together from fundraisers and other events. But they stand far apart on one big topic: Crime. There has to be more to it. There's a brief moment we even stop talking and just focus on reading over the new information.

"Are you seeing the same connections I am?"

"I think so, Marie, but I'm not quite sure it looks the same through my eyes. Why don't you explain it first?"

He's funny.

"Okay, the father of the missing girl. That councilman is newer to the seat, whereas

Councilman Schwartz has been in his seat for some time. My guess is that he used his veteran leadership pull to coax this young guy along and get him to do some shady shit and make some easy money. When I took the money and it went missing, Andy freaked out. He needed a fall guy and some control. I would only assume the other councilman wanted to turn themselves in or call the cops. Andy knew it would get figured out eventually and didn't want to call anyone. He turned a bad storm into a shit storm. Schwartz is making this worse by the minute. He's like a teenager telling worse lies every day to cover up shitty lies to his parents."

"Okay, that was more detail than I had. I was going to say he pressured him. That's all I had, though." Christian smiled.

"Off-topic, Christian, where are you staying in town?" I asked.

"Actually, in the Quarter, thanks to the combination of Uncle Sam paying and Neil. I parked up the street from your place, though. Why don't we head out of here and walk there?"

"Sounds good. I'm getting tired after today."

Walking back to my place, I keep looking at him, gazing into the distance like a lost schoolgirl. It's been a rough couple of weeks, and he's a calming influence in my life right now. I can't mess this up and go jump in bed with him. I know if I offered it to him, he'd come eagerly. I'm not saying I don't want to. There is a part of me telling my heart and brain to shut the front door and just have a great time with him.

Within sight of my place, he leans in and kisses me on the cheek and puts his arm over my shoulders. For a moment, a brief moment, I feel safe from all the crazy shit I get myself into. In many ways, he reminds me of my father; he's got that same drive, military feel, and he's big. He has a big chest, big arms and big heart; this dude is going to be bad for business, I can already tell.

As I turn and begin walking up to my place, I look back, and he isn't looking. Just as I begin to open the door, I can see him glancing at me as I walk inside. Knowing he looked back gives me goosebumps. It brings me back to high school when I'd try to get the attention of a crush.

I think it's going to take some time before the possibility of us getting together, which might end up making it even harder since we could end up in that awkward friend zone. It's a risk I'm going to take; I need to focus on this case, and I need his help.

Tired and mentally drained, I sit down on the couch to take off my shoes. It's a bad idea that turns into me passing out right then and there, caving into the warm embrace of the cushions. As I fall asleep, drifting off into the land of dreams, I'm met with Christian's face.

8

"To be safe in these situations, it's about planning and strategizing."

I t's not too long before I wake up with a sudden urge to do something. I tend to wake up abruptly and a bit abrasively while my mind creates new questions for me to solve. I have yet to get the Neil Baggio epiphany; instead, I get the Marie Perdita quandary.

As I wake up from a dead sleep, I can't help but break out my phone and check my email. Rule number one if you wake up in the middle of the night: Don't look at your phone. It's as if you are opening your very own Pandora's box of sleep distractions. I roll over, squint my eyes, and see two things. The first is that my phone was about to die. The second is an email from TJ with results of the background search he and the FBI pulled up on the case.

As I sit up on the couch, I see it's almost four in the morning. I only got about two hours of sleep on a stiff couch. Needless to say, I'm feeling a bit rough right now. I take my phone to the room, plug it in to charge, and grab my tablet to start going over the email and documents they sent over. With nervous energy, I decide to start my morning routine, which means Flintstone vitamins along with my pre-workout supplements and a big glass of water to wash it all down.

I throw on some shorts and a tee and hop on the bike. With my tablet in hand, I put on some music and start to ride. It dawns on me that this case was going to need some crazy red yarn, just like Sherlock's board.

There is something to be said about being tactile and having the ability to visualize the connections. I do a similar thing, just in an app. It is the digital age, after all, and this way I can bring my crazy with me. As I said earlier, I use sales software to track down and organize leads on people, just like a sales rep would. The difference is that I use it to track drug dealers, killers, and overall bad guys. For connecting the dots, though, I go a bit old school. I use a simple Excel spreadsheet that allows me to move people around. It works for me and allows me to quickly hide my crazy thoughts.

After a few hours, I start to crash from the lack of sleep mixed with the mental drain of studying at four in the morning. I'm going to need to get a nap in or finish sleeping if I'm going to be of any use today. I simply flop down on the bed, not even under the covers. It's an old trick I've picked up over the years when I need a nap. If I get under the covers like I'm normally sleeping, I'll crash. If I simply lay on top, I'll get some rest then wake up from being uncomfortable.

After a few hours of sleep, I hear a pounding at the door. I'm assuming it's Christian at this point since I have a few missed calls from him, according to my phone. I'm struggling to swipe through notifications as I stumble to the door. Wait a minute, one of these texts is from Christian saying he's downtown working on a lead, something about the chief of police.

I grab my gun from the coffee table and make my way toward the door. Who the hell is here then? Shit, it's LT and Andy—what do they want? Time to open the door and put on a smile, play dumb, and hope for the best.

"Hey, LT . . . Andy . . . What can I do for you two gents this morning?"

"Aren't you going to welcome us in?" Andy is a real prick.

"Well, I'm not sure how you know where I live, and I'm not dressed. Can you tell me what this is about? A head's up would have been nice." I have an idea.

"Why don't you let us in and we can talk?" LT tries to help.

"Tell you what, how about you let a girl have some privacy, get ready, and meet you for coffee? Otherwise, I can simply shoot your buddy LT in the leg, laugh a bit and call the cops. Your choice. I'm not a fan of being left to hold the bag and then surprised the next morning as if nothing happened."

"That's why I'm here. I want to apologize for the way things ended last night." Look at Andy, trying to be suave.

"Let me ask you a question then, since you aren't a fan of them being dicks last night."

"Shoot, what can I answer for you? I'm just trying to move this thing along."

"Did you bring flowers? That's always a nice gesture when a man does something stupid to a girl."

"No, I did not. Tell you what, LT and I will go get some flowers for you while you get ready. Give you like thirty minutes?"

"Make them white lilies and give me forty-five minutes. Otherwise, your buddy LT might still get shot." I plaster on a smile.

"We'll be back in a few with some flowers. You have my humblest of apologies."

I don't even say goodbye; I simply shut the door in his face. Sometimes men like Andy are so used to getting their way that you can throw them off. Give them a little misdirection, don't let them have what they crave. Then, it makes them want it more. It's funny to watch powerful men act like little boys. I go into the bathroom with my gun close, in case these idiots try to kick in the door.

If I have to, I'll shoot them dead in their tracks naked as a newborn baby. They'd probably be distracted. I could just walk up and pistol-whip them. Over the next fifteen minutes, I showered and dried my hair fast; it was quick even for me. I wanted to make sure I had time to relax, regroup, and plant some guns in different places, like the kitchen or bathroom. To be safe in these situations, it's about planning and strategizing. You can't go driving a car through a police station like someone I know. There's the knock at the door. It's time to play nice.

"Who is it?" I was acting playful.

"You know who it is. We come with gifts this time." Andy was trying.

As I opened the door, I acted surprised. If I was going to put on a show, it was going to be Oscar-worthy. I'm not going to waste my time and half-ass it for these boys. I did just demand that they go get flowers for me.

"Flowers, for me? And they're lilies, my favorite!"

"Very funny, Marie. Can we come in now?" Andy was agitated.

"Sure, it's not every day a gentleman brings a lady some beautiful flowers." I smile to show my appreciation.

"You're one special girl, Marie, that's for sure." Ah, LT called me a girl, not a woman or lady.

"Well, boys, what can I do for you?"

"We need to go over last night; we also need to talk about how you might be able to help us with an issue we're struggling to deal with." Andy scowls.

LT perks up. "Yeah, with the way you handled yourself last night, we think your skills and ingenuity are just what we need for this problem."

"Well, what can I do for you?"

As Andy and LT come in and sit down on the couch, I'm forced to grab a kitchen table chair. Seating is minimal in this place; I'm still a bit ticked they found me so quickly, but I'm not surprised. I'll deal with that shit later. For now, I need to work on this relationship and overall dynamic.

Andy begins talking and going over the issue of the missing money, as well as the need to track down who did it. He and LT aren't quite sure whether it was an inside job, since there weren't a lot of people that knew what he was up to. Little do they know, the search will be short since I'm the one that took it. They go over what happened and what they are doing to rectify the situation; it takes a good hour, but I think I get the gist of it.

"OK, let me get this straight: You need *my* help with something *this* big?"

"We're in a bind." LT's more obvious than Andy.

"You borrowed some money from the city. You were going to use it to fund the purchase and sale of some products. Then you were going to return the money before anyone found out. It turns out, someone did find out and reported it missing. Now you are asking me, since I'm on the outside and resourceful, to look into this for you?"

You can just see the desperation on Andy's face. He was worried about his crew and upset that he had to throw something like this at me. They all act big, want to scare you, and it often works. The problem is when the woman on the other side of the conversation has more experience at being a badass than you do. Andy and LT are decent bad guys, but they are butterflies compared to the likes of Gaines. That guy is creepy and nuts to the millionth degree. I'm still haunted by the time that

I was on the other side of Neil and his team trying to infiltrate Gaines's organization for the CIA. It was a disaster. These guys are local thugs trying to cover their tracks and doing a shit job of it. I'm not saying they wouldn't have gotten away with it, had I not been involved. I'm just saying they're low-rent.

"That's pretty much it in a nutshell. Do you have any other questions?"

"Do you know who reported the money stolen?" My bet is the guy with the missing daughter.

"No, we just know it's someone on the City Council with me." I smell bullshit.

"Well, I guess I can do this for you, but what do I get for it, another five bucks?"

"How about a finder's fee of ten percent?" Or all of it, since it's in my bank account.

"That sounds fair. I'll see what I can come up with in the meantime. If I'm snooping around a city building, police station, et cetera, just know I'm looking into this for you."

"Understood, we appreciate your willingness to help." LT breathes a sigh of relief.

"It's going to be the best place to start."

"I agree, Andy. May I ask you one final question?"

"Sure, at this point, anything goes." Andy says,

smiling.

"How long have you tailed me? It's not like anyone knows I'm here."

"After last night, we had Charlie keep an eye out for your car when you got back into town. Then he followed you back here last night. He said you had a nice gentleman walk you home, but he didn't come in. Is he a friend of yours?"

"No, just a guy I met. We went on a quick date, nothing major. Just a single girl in a cool town." Will they buy it?

"I can't judge anyone with my past. If you look into this, please don't involve anyone else outside of the crew."

"No problem. You guys have a great day. I know how to get ahold of LT if I find anything."

"Feel free to contact me directly. LT will give you my information."

Just like that, I escort the two guys out of my apartment and get Andy's cell phone information. This will allow Uncle Phil and our other contacts to track his movements. It's a start. It also gives me coverage to be more brazen in my investigation. They will think I'm snooping around for them, not on them. I'll be honest: I work my ass off to get leads, but sometimes good old-fashioned luck can carry you far in this work.

But you need to create that luck by putting

yourself in the right situations. I need to reach out to Christian and see what he has going on downtown after I email this updated info to Phil. He's here to help, but he's also here to keep an eye on me. I'm not blind to the fact that my freedom is tied to his reporting of my good deeds.

I shoot Christian a text asking him to call me when he's free. For now, I head out for a quick run to clear my head and stay loose.

About a mile into my run, I see Christian calling.

"Hey Christian, if you hear me breathing heavy, it's because I'm running."

"From somebody or for exercise?"

"Exercise, but I did get a visit this morning from Andy and LT at my place."

"What the . . . I'm assuming you're okay and everything worked out?"

"Yeah, they asked me to look into the person who stole their money. The easy part is finding the truth, I stole it. The hard part is finding the plausible solution that doesn't get someone else killed. What do you have going on downtown?"

"Thanks to that email TJ and Ken sent over last night, we can connect the chief of police and Andy. I went downtown to catch the councilman whose daughter is missing for some information. We had a quick chat, but he said he would call me later to talk outside of work."

"With everything going on, how'd you get that meeting?"

"Mike called the local FBI office assigned to aid in the case and gave them the green light to let me talk to him. That opened the door for him trusting me pretty quick."

"As for the connection, I think I know what you're talking about. I was reading that Andy and the police chief went to high school together and are in touch all over social media."

"Not only that, but this morning TJ reported multiple transfers of large sums of money from one of Andy's companies to the police chief's sister."

"I love how people think they're so slick sometimes." Not everyone can be on my level.

"I know, it's not hard if you just stay on the trail and follow the breadcrumbs. Like Neil always says, it's about finding the possibilities and then crossing them off one at a time."

Christian and I spend the next couple of minutes going over details from the case while I run back to the house. Once back, I quickly clean up, throw on my uniform—the incognito outfit of tight jeans, a hoodie and a hat to hide my face— and head out to do some digging of my own. Christian thinks we can meet up with the father in the Quarter. He's trying to set up dinner or drinks and will text me, he says.

While he does that, I'm heading down to the police department to look into some other stuff. I should probably call Andy and see if he can get me access to the station, or at least the files related to the stolen money.

"Hey Andy, it's Marie. Can you do me a quick favor?"

"Depends on what it is."

"Can you get me access to the police station, and what little info they might have on the case of the missing money?"

"Do you have a backstory you think you can use to be less conspicuous?"

"You could tell them you hired a private investigator from out of state that specializes in this type of thing to help out. Then you look like you're cooperating and trying to help."

"I can do that. Give me fifteen minutes, and I'll get it rolling."

"Perfect, it should take me about thirty minutes to head that way."

Making my way to the police station from my place doesn't take long. I'm driving through New Orleans in my Wrangler, listening to some Miles Davis today, according to the DJ. I know there are satellite channels for jazz, but there is something great about a local New Orleans DJ giving you the background on each track. It's humid, and as bugs whip by me, I can feel a few of them hit my hair.

This drive is making me second-guess the old open-air Wrangler. That, and all the rain they get out here. The soft top is in the back, but it's pretty torn up. Maybe I'll find a way to rig just the top to have some cover. With my focus fading in and out, I eventually arrive at my destination. Andy has things all set up.

Ask for Officer Mike Moore. He'll take care of you.

I walk into the precinct looking like a woman scorned, with a shit expression on my face. I keep getting looks from the officers, judging me, trying to see what I'm up to. I also have a backpack on with a hat pulled over my face. I'm not giving off a Nancy Drew or Kitty Forman type of vibe.

The officer at the front desk looks old as can be; he's a short man, stocky, like your crazy uncle at Christmas. His hair had that salt and pepper look to it, but I couldn't tell if he was actually old, or the job made him that way.

"Hello, ma'am, what can I do for you?"

"My name is Marie; I was told by the Councilman a Mike Moore would be able to help me."

"That would actually be me. I just spoke to Mr. Schwartz. He said you'd be over shortly. I haven't had time to put the file together, but if you take a seat, I can get started on it."

"If it's going to take you a while, I can come back later. I don't want to intrude on your day."

"Ma'am . . . Marie, don't be silly. I can get it for you, just be patient and sit in the lobby."

Sitting in the entryway of a New Orleans police precinct is fun; it's almost like being on an episode of HBO's *Taxicab Confessions*. There are some fascinating people in here. Take, for example, the lady sitting next to me; she has a neck tattoo of a Ford F-150 on the right side under her ear, not even done with a background, stylish, or anything. She doesn't even have the hillbilly banner, confederate flag, tattooed somewhere visible. I say that because one would expect that kind of person to get a truck neck tattoo.

Remember, when I speak of tattoos, I have plenty. Hell, I'm working on a sleeve of my own. My right arm is covered in an Asian tapestry; I know it's cliché, but it's not your generic type of work with koi or a snake. It's my life, the things that are important to me, hidden in a tattoo. It allows me to remember who I am when I'm playing all these characters.

As I sat there next to the truck neck lady, I realize something. Officer Moore hasn't gotten up or moved since I walked over here. Hell, it almost looks like he's sleeping. I guess I better settle in, get to know some of my neighbors, and do one of those "lost in my own thoughts" things.

I open my bag and grab some headphones and my tablet. I figure if I'm going to be here, I might as well get some work done, take some notes and do some tree-building; it's like gardening but with a case. You start with a section of people and work your way back to the trunk. It allows you to see how people are connected to the case, if at all.

Yep, Officer Moore's asleep. I watch another officer stick a pencil in his hand, and he doesn't budge. He's out cold. At this point, I wonder if he's dead.

9

"Did I miss something?"

I have been able to accomplish a lot of work in a short period of time, making today a decent one in my book. I opened up my internet radio app and started playing a jazz stream. I have to admit, jazz is growing on me. After listening to music and working for an hour, I notice truck neck tattoo lady—or "TNT lady," as I will now call her—left for a few and just came back. The difference is now she wants to talk to me. This should be fun.

"Hey, whatcha listening to?" TNT lady says.

"Just some jazz while I'm trying to get some work done."

"You've been sitting here an awfully long time. What are you in for? They catch you working a corner?" Shit, do I look like a hooker?

"No, I'm here to get something that a friend said was waiting for me. They just don't have it yet, so I'm waiting."

"You might be waiting for a long time then. Nothing happens fast in the south, and it definitely doesn't happen fast in New Orleans."

"I'll keep that in mind and try to be patient. What are you doing here? Waiting for someone?"

"Sort of. My man got pinched last night. I'm trying to post bail, but don't have enough money."

"That sucks, is he okay?"

"Yeah, he's been in and out of prison, like me most of my life. I just don't have the three grand for bail."

"How short are you?" I'm not offering to help, just curious.

"Well, I don't know. I have twenty dollars, so how short am I?"

"I'd say all of it since you probably need that twenty bucks." I smile.

"Damn straight. I think I'm just going to have to let him sit in there." She chuckles.

We go back and forth for a little bit and got to know each other. Well, she gets to know the character I'm playing here in New Orleans. I start to realize she may be a little off her rocker. Still, she's keenly aware and observant of the situation and people here. She knows most of the officers, the inner workings of the precinct, and most notably the cops she can work with.

What she means by that are cops that will work with her or her man to share intel on other crimes. The cops look at them like the minnows in a pond, only useful for catching bigger fish, but they're involved in a lot of environments where more serious crimes happen. Since they look like a small-time dealer and his hooker girlfriend, no one pays them attention. That also means they have an understanding of what's going on with the police and criminal interactions.

Part of me feels like I'm talking to a conspiracy fangirl, but she's giving me things to look into. She's a starting point; even if she's a bit crazy, she has some information she's working with. Often when investigating, you might find a witness who might not be great in court. That witness, though, can be a starting point to the path that gets the needed evidence.

When I look at cases like this, it's about compiling data and connections I can put into my digital tree and work backward. Some won't connect and will simply be outliers; others lead me in the direction where I need to be. The kind of work I do, infiltrating organizations, starts with creating a persona, which allows me access.

I spent a few hours in and out of thought,

thinking about the time in Detroit with Gaines and how it led me to Santa Fe. All of that shit, all of those choices, led me here; it felt like I was drifting in and out of memories, when I realized I was dreaming. I had passed out without a single word from my buddy Officer Moore. Even TNT lady was gone; I had dozed off. Everything had finally caught up to me. I got up and walked over there, only to find out he was no longer at his desk. I waved over another police officer behind the counter.

"Sir, where did Officer Moore go?"

"Officer Moore went on lunch. Is there anything I can help you with?"

"He was supposed to get me a packet of information for a case I'm helping to investigate for the City Council. I specialize in insurance and money laundering cases. They brought me in to try and find that missing money."

"Is your name Marie by any chance?"

"Yes, it is. How'd you know?"

"I didn't. There's just an envelope on his desk that says 'For Marie.' Here you go. Can I do anything else for you?"

"No. Thank you for your help."

As I began walking back to my Jeep, I started to review the past two hours. Did I miss something? Did he call for me and I just not hear him? Maybe he forgot I was in the lobby; maybe he forgot I was even here, and he had it waiting for me when I showed up. I had to file it under "Deal with It Later." For now, I'm going to go through this packet and see what I can come up with.

I just need to find somewhere to sit down and enjoy a bit of commotion and distraction. I think better with a little bit of chaos. It's not surprising, when you think about all the exercises my father had me do. If it's too quiet, I get lost in my own thoughts. I decide to text Christian and see what time we're meeting with the father of the missing girl. For a change, he responds quickly. "Drago's by the casino at five p.m."

I guess I'll try to stay on that side of town. That way, if I get carried away, I'll be close by. There are plenty of great places to eat and drink off Poydras. I think I can go to Bourbon Street, which might end poorly, or I can go to Mother's, walking distance from the restaurant. I can grab something small to eat, hang out, and work. Then I won't feel the need to stuff my face with chargrilled oysters; they're so good. The first time I ever ate there, I think I split four dozen with a friend of mine; I've learned not to go hungry ever since.

It was oddly slow at Mother's Restaurant. I'll take it, though; I need some time to work and don't want a server kicking me out. This place is usually hopping. Rarely do you walk in here and not have to deal with a long line. I might have to tip the staff early and significantly to keep them off my back. I went for the famous ham sandwich; can't go wrong with that. Plus, I'm hoping that and a ton of water mixed with another pre-workout pill will have me rocking the rest of the day.

As I sit down at a small table along the wall reviewing documents that became more and more useless with each turn of the page, my phone goes off. I wonder what Andy is calling me about . . . maybe to check up.

"Hey, Marie, how's it going? Were you able to get any leads from Officer Moore?"

"First off, was I getting punked, or is that really your go-to guy?"

"I'm pretty sure he's losing it; that's why I sent you to him. He'd get the info for me and not ask questions. Let me guess, he forgot about you or fell asleep?"

"Try both, but I got something from another officer that he had put together for me."

"Is there anything of use in there?"

"As of right now, nope. But he accidentally gave me a few sheets on the missing girl case. Do the police think they're related?" I don't know if he did; I'm just fishing.

"No, they shouldn't be. I mean, they didn't say anything. Haven't said anything." He's starting to stammer a bit and get agitated.

"I didn't mean to upset you. You want me looking at the money case, so I'll toss this. Don't worry. I won't spend another moment on it." On this probably make-believe paper I haven't seen yet.

"Thank you, Marie, for your understanding. I get worked up because I knew that missing girl. Her father and I work together. I have a son, so I can only imagine what it would be like if someone kidnapped him."

"It's okay, I understand. I'll let you know if I find anything, I promise. I'm just getting started, so it's going to take me at least a day or two to hopefully connect some dots, but I'll see what I can do."

"Good luck!" His voice was still shaky.

"Talk to you later, sir."

I don't know what to call him. I'll just go with the simple approach and say "sir." For now I need to keep hoping there is something in here that relates to the missing girl or her father connecting the dots. For now I have my tablet open but I'm not able to add many notes.

This went on for a few hours until I realize it's almost five and I'm going to be late. I shoot a text to Christian to let him know my ETA, pack up my stuff, and head out. As I was walking fast, damn near running, something on one of the sheets stuck out in my brain. I was so concerned with looking for leads I could use to distract from the money I stole that I didn't notice the councilman's name all over those reports. The man I'm about to meet, the one whose daughter is missing. He's the one that blew the whistle on the missing money. He knows something more that he isn't letting on. I can feel it.

As I walked in, I see Christian and the councilman. I can only imagine what it would be like dealing with this. It has to be a mix of emotions, especially if you feel it's tied to something you did. Even if it was the right thing, it has consequences now. Hopefully they won't be as dire as my actions with Agent Garcia, even if I felt they were right at the time.

"Hey Marie, how are you doing? This is Councilman Wes Rivers. He's the one with the missing daughter, Leslie."

"From the paperwork I just saw, you're also the one that blew the whistle on the missing money from the city?"

"Yes, I am. That's why I wanted to talk to you outside of my office or anywhere near law enforcement. You can never be too careful. I did some digging on Christian and his company, BCI. You are hard to find anything on. Is that on purpose?"

"Yes, it's by design. Do you still want my help, knowing I'm essentially a ghost?"

"I need all the help I can get. I know who has my daughter, but there's nothing I can do about it."

"Do you mean Andy the Brat?"

"You mean Councilman Schwartz? But yes, as they are one and the same."

"I had the pleasure of meeting him recently. He's struggling to figure out how to solve this money issue, isn't he?" I have to play it close to the vest.

"You mean the money he originally stole, then lost?" He's getting visibly upset.

"You know, why don't we slow down and start at the beginning?" Christian steps in to calm him down.

"Okay, I can do that. I just get worked up. I want my baby girl back."

"We can understand that. Marie is great at what she does. We will do our best to help you out."

We spend the next twenty minutes talking in circles, with him giving us many details we already knew, but us having to play coy so as to not give away the depths of our connection to Andy and his crew. I have to do it for his protection—and mine, let's be honest. I would love to help him and his daughter, but I can't do it if I'm dead. As the conversation continues, we speak about the case and how Wes got involved. Wes is a slender man— early fifties, I would guess. He has a full beard, and his hair has turned gray, perhaps quicker than normal under the circumstances. When this started, I thought the missing girl was young or small. But as we spoke, I realized she is in high school. She is about to be a senior showing promise in her studies and athletics.

As if it isn't hard enough dealing with losing a child, it being one with such great potential and the world at her fingertips has to be brutal. You can hear the way he describes her with the utmost admiration. He is proud of his daughter and what she has accomplished.

"Wes, please don't take this the wrong way. I understand you miss your daughter, but we keep getting derailed with her and not how or why she's missing. What was and is your relationship with Schwartz and the money that was stolen?" I'm losing my patience.

"I guess I've beaten around the bush enough. Schwartz and I came up with this plan more than a year ago. When it came time to move the money, sell the drugs, and then put it back, I got cold feet and backed out. We left it at that, or so I thought.

He eventually got up the nerve to do it on his own. I told him not to do it, to keep me and the city out of it. I thought he heeded my advice."

"Then you noticed the money missing and felt compelled to report it. I don't think you were trying to throw him under the bus. You just weren't about to let the city lose that money, and now he's pissed at you and using your daughter as leverage to keep you quiet. At least, that's my guess."

"That's the gist of it, Marie. I just want my daughter back. I'm not about to do anything to him. I don't trust he won't come after me if I do. I regret the decision every day to report the loss. I was afraid I would get blamed for the money."

"We will see what we can come up with. Marie and I will get to work and keep you out of it."

"Guys, if you can excuse me a minute, I need to wash up." I had a missed call from Diego.

As I walk back to the bathroom, I duck down and quickly make myself hard to see from outside. Something didn't seem right. Maybe I was overreacting. Maybe I was paranoid. I don't know. Then again, that attitude has kept me alive. I shoot Christian a text message to keep an eye out for Diego's crew, then I move to dip out through the kitchen. As I slip inside, the chef yells.

"Ma'am, you can't be in here!"

"Sorry, sir, my date is really weird, and honestly, he's huge. I don't want him to think I left. I just need a quiet way out of here. Is there a back door?" I smile and act scared, though I feel my heart pounding.

"This way, miss. Sorry for startling you. Giuseppi, show her out the back door." He quickly turned into a gentleman.

"Thank you, sir. By the way, I love this place. Your restaurant is divine." He smiles as I quickly duck out the back door.

Christian has sent me a flurry of messages letting me know a few cars were dropping off guys out front.

The call from Diego was probably to see if you had answered inside.

I take that lead and shoot Diego a message telling him I was busy on a date. Then he gets cute, saying it couldn't be that great if I'm texting him. Before I know it, he's flirting with me as I'm running through alleys, ducking in and out of hotels, trying to make sure no one sees me.

I hear a commotion in the streets, yelling and what sounds like guys trying to organize. Again, this is New Orleans, so that could simply be a second line or a bachelor party. That's not a chance I can take. With Andy showing up at my place, LT and Charlie working right by me, and all of this so close to home, I need to disappear for a little bit and think.

I have a new lead, Wes Rivers and his missing girl. He reported the missing funds because he didn't want to get caught up in Schwartz's mess, and now his daughter is kidnapped. This keeps getting thicker. I know everyone likes to think of the world like a movie or a book, but life isn't that way. We all know that shit. Bad people get away with shit because they fall into it. It's happenstance, then they ride that wave until it kills them, or they mess up so bad they get caught. That's why the ones like the BTK killer go so long without ever getting captured.

I settle into the Westin hotel lobby with my documents and a bottle of water. I tip the bartender handsomely to leave me alone and act like I am a real paying customer, not just some lady drinking water and sifting through paperwork, trying to hide from some goons. At least for now, even if they find me, I have a good story. I'm trying to find out who is behind this money thing that Andy wants me to look into. The problem is, I know that's bullshit. I'm just trying to find a way into this case that keeps me out of it and a way to get the money back to the city, all while rescuing another lost girl. The bartender keeps looking at me as if I am overstaying my welcome, which is fine because my phone rings. It isn't a number I know.

"Go for Marie. What can I do for you?" I begin packing my stuff up.

"Hey, this is Diego. Where are you at? And why haven't you called me back from earlier?" He sounds a bit mad.

"Is a girl not allowed to go on a date? I had spent most of my day running around doing work I was asked to, and now I'm getting shit from you. I'm finishing up at the Westin, just reviewing some information I had to go over."

"Who was asking you to do what?" Shit, did Andy and LT keep Diego out of the loop?

I might have stepped into it; there is a way I can save this. Diego has to know. I think he's just mad at me for not answering the phone. He and Andy are used to controlling things. At least they have the illusion of control. They are half-assing their way through this; well, Diego not so much. He seems to have his hands around his role. On the other hand, Andy is just some spoiled guy who wants more and thinks he's untouchable.

"Diego, first of all, I don't remember some initiation that said I was now your property and must answer to you and your crew. Second, you are fully aware of who I was trying to meet and how he operates. If you are in the dark on something, I say ask your crew. Don't get on me."

Crossing my fingers that this works.

"Who do you think is on my ass? If you last long enough, someday, I can give you the rundown of how this thing works. For now, you better be there. LT is coming to pick you up."

"Tell you what. LT can come to take a picture of me at the Westin to make Andy happy. Then tell Andy he can either trust me or not. Better yet, I'm done with this task. Especially after that shit at the warehouse. You boys can keep your games."

"Hold up! Slow down. I'm just playing my part, just like you are. LT is walking in, he'll take a pic, make Andy happy, and you can get out of there and do what you want. I'll deal with Andy. He often forgets he can't control everyone all the time." No shit!

Diego spends the next couple minutes talking vaguely to me, trying to calm me down and sweet-talk me. It's a different side of him. He isn't flirting, but almost doing damage control a bit. You could feel he was used to cleaning up Andy's messes. LT walks in, grabs me by the arm, and I give him the look of death.

"What the hell do you think you are doing?" I say.

"My job. You're coming with me." He tries to drag me out the door.

"If I were you, I'd answer your phone."

"This is LT. Yeah, Diego, I'm here . . . What? . . . You sure? . . . If you say so."

LT slowly lets go, looks at me, snaps a quick picture, then flips me the bird. He's pissed. I'm not sure at which part the most, but it doesn't matter. I went from almost getting seen with the missing girl's father and Christian again, blowing our cover, to pissing off Andy, Diego and LT. Now I should be back to square one, which is what it's like in my life. I need to get back to my place, clean up and drop this stuff off.

10

"Did you tell her about the yacht?"

The night's a bit of a bust; neither LT nor
Charlie is working. I'm able to get word to
LT and find out if there is anything I can help with
the next couple of days, though. After we go back
and forth a few times, he says he'll have Charlie
reach out to me in the morning to see if I can help
with some local errands for Andy and the crew.

I reach out to Christian next. We had spoken
earlier when I was walking to the bar, but I think
it'll be nice to spend more time getting to know
him. Also, I'm dressed up and want to flirt with a
guy, someone I find interesting. It doesn't hurt that
he plays the handsome knight in shining armor
quite well. I send him a text asking him to head
toward Bourbon Street for a bit of decompressing

and talking. We'll meet at Pat O'Brien's to listen to some music, do some drinking, and enjoy the courtyard. I know it's not his usual vibe, but he still says he'll come out like the gentleman he is.

Pat O'Brien's in the quarter is a favorite with tourists and locals. The tall green doors surrounded by a reddish-orange building can be seen from across town. Okay, maybe you can't see it from that far, but it's very noticeable. The doorman doesn't even ask for my ID, which gives me a bit of a sour taste. Not sure why, but I'm in a mood today. I'm just dying a bit, feeling lonely and needing some attention. I don't want it from just any random guy, like the two guys across the bar already sizing me up like a T-bone.

Guys, for those of you reading this, let me give you a quick piece of advice. When you see a gorgeous woman you want to approach, there is a fine line between confidence and creepy. Remember, less is more. It will be easy to see when you are confident, so don't force it.

Back to these jerkoffs slowly making their way towards me. They're stalking me across the bar. It's not subtle or smooth by any means, but sloppy by design, like drunken boxing. You could see that they've tried this move on more than one girl before. I can't wait to see where this is going. I'm standing at the bar, waiting to order a drink when they finally approach me.

"Hey, babe, what's a beautiful bombshell like you doing at a bar alone?" Should I tell them a massive man is on his way to meet me? Nah!

"I'm just out having some fun. I moved here for work, figured what better way to meet new people than to go out. What are you two guys doing besides acting a bit sloppy?" My smile quickly turns to a stare as I see the other guy continually adjust himself.

"Just like you, we're out looking for some fun. Why don't the three of us get to know each other? Maybe get out of here to somewhere quieter?" Is this dude for real?

"Well, you haven't even introduced yourself, but thanks for the offer. I'm good."

I turn to the bartender to order two hurricanes. I mean, we're here, might as well enjoy the local drinking scene. Tweedledee and Tweedledumber are still standing there, confused that I'm not swept off my feet by their fantastic offer of drunk sex with two strangers.

"Hey babe, you didn't have to order me a drink." I slap his hand away from grabbing the glass.

"These aren't for you, but nice try. I'm meeting a friend. You guys should probably walk away."

"If you have another friend coming, we can

make it a party then. The more, the merrier." His friend just sits there while he runs his mouth.

"Well, *he's* not up for that kind of party, and neither am I. Why not go and have a good time with someone else? Have a great night, guys."

I take the two drinks and find my way into the courtyard to look for a table, somewhere Christian and I can sit and talk. I can see out of the corner of my eye those two guys are still staring at me like a high-priced steak dinner. They won't take no for an answer, and I really don't want to get these clothes dirty beating up two assholes tonight.

I got pretty to flirt and have some fun, not to deal with two poor excuses for humans on any level. It didn't seem to stop them that I was ignoring their attempt to get my attention from across the room. It looks as if the quiet one's going to take a shot. He's worked up enough courage to talk to me and crosses the bar to my table.

"Hey babe, I don't think you understand what you're turning down. We have an awesome apartment downtown, a yacht parked in the marina. This could be a night you'll remember forever. Have you ever been on a yacht?" Oh geez, this is his best attempt?

"Let me make this clear to you. I'm not going anywhere with you or your friend. Just walk away and let me be. You really don't want me to get up and embarrass you two in front of a whole bar." He waves his friend over.

"Hey, bro, this bitch is telling us she can kick our ass." I went from babe to bitch in two minutes; that's a new personal best!

"So, this whore is too cool to hang out with us? Did you tell her about the yacht?" Way to try and save it.

"Ok, I'm going to get up now and give you one last warning before I kick both your teeth in."

All of a sudden, the two of them look white as ghosts and stop all the bullshit. Their demeanor goes from cocky prick to shy child. That's when I turn around and see Christian standing there with a t-shirt tight enough to look like he stole it from me. Don't get me wrong, he looks sexy as hell in it, but it's still tight.

"Guys, I think you should listen to the lady. Have a great night! Marie, you good?"

Christian stood up behind them, barrel chest and all. Though I was looking forward to making fools of them, it was fun being rescued for a change. The two men quickly turned to boys, trying to fake interest in something on the other side of the bar. One of them even went as far as pulling the fake phone call routine. I could see the one guy's heart in his throat. That's the presence a guy like Christian has. Sometimes I'm envious of that. However, it would make the "hiding in plain sight" part of my job difficult.

"I was going to embarrass them, but thanks for the backup, as usual. A girl can get used to a strong guy like you constantly showing up to save her, even if I don't need it."

"It's in my nature. Want to sit down?"

"Yes, I got us some hurricanes to try. I'm not a big drinker anyway, but I thought it would be a nice thing to share." Who am I kidding? I can drink like a frat boy.

"I'm game. It's been a long day anyways, could use a bit of decompressing. How'd the rest of your day go?"

We sit there talking for a good hour before we even touch the drinks. It's loud, a crazy New Orleans night with people all around us. Despite my best efforts to flirt with him, I'm getting nothing in return. I'm laughing gently at his jokes. I'm subtly touching his arm, even his shoulder, and looking into his eyes. Either he isn't into me at all, or he's just that clueless.

Most men don't realize how hard it is to be a girl, especially when it comes to flirting with or trying to date the opposite sex. Guys can be clueless. It's so hard to tell if you're just not into us or you're blind to what's going on. I remember one of my last boyfriends in college—Chad Damons was his name. He was oblivious, even for a guy who came off smooth. Just thinking of it has me laughing and getting a bit angry inside. Laughing for him, crying for me.

As the night went on, I find myself a bit buzzed from that one drink and having only eaten that ham sandwich and some oysters throughout the day. I'm also pretty sure these drinks are half rum; they pour to party down here. I keep trying to get his attention without making it blatantly obvious, but I realize after an hour of flirting this is going nowhere.

"Christian, let me get this straight. According to what you're saying, we both came to the same conclusion. The police chief looks clean, but it looks like someone else close to him is making moves for his office?"

"Yes, but I'm not sure how I can confirm it. I'm also not sure how I'm going to find out who's involved. TJ is already looking for a way to move the money around that you took and get it back to the city. That's just another piece to this puzzle."

"Well, between the two of us, we can figure it out. I'll call an old newspaper contact and see if they can help me touch base with the police chief to judge his reaction."

"Do you mean Jim from Ann Arbor? I remember him talking to Neil a couple of times while we were searching for you."

"The very same one. Hopefully he's not too pissed about me lying to him and running off."

"He got the story and then some because of you. I think he'll just be happy you're alive and well. Also, you're not a villain, like we all thought for a minute."

"Easier said than done, but I'll try him in the morning."

After a good fifteen minutes on the endless possibilities of who could be steering the police chief's office and working with Andy, Christian just blurted it out. It caught me off guard, and I'm not sure why. He has every right to ask and know why or what happened that day.

"Hey Marie, can I ask you something? How did it come to you and Agent Garcia? I mean what would have put you in that place? Why not try and save her?"

"I guess you deserve the truth."

I guess everyone deserves to know what happened, how I got put in that situation. When I reached out to Maria for help, I was grasping at straws. It was my half-court three-pointer to try to win the game. When she took me in, worked with me, and saw hope in me, I felt something that had been missing for some time. Even my final year on good terms with the agency was rough. I was on an island, often a leaf in the wind, holding on for dear life to its tree limb.

Maria had seen that fear in my eyes, that desperation, and decided to help me. She told me it would be hard to get Neil on board. He might not even come around. After a week of working and talking with Neil and Maria, I felt things were coming together and that I might get support back. The life I have led doesn't allow me a mulligan. I'm not allowed to start over, go back, and enjoy my life. I'm lost to my family forever. It's just a matter of how they will find out I'm gone. I've upset too many people; if I go back to my family, I put them at risk. Maria understood that, saw my need for family, for friends, and embraced me. That's what made this whole situation so difficult.

While working the case, we had a meeting with Susie Gaines, some drug cartel leaders, and Ms. Choike. Maria was supposed to stay outside and simply listen in from the car. I had a wire on; it was small, but it was still there. While we were walking in, I noticed they were searching everyone with a metal detector wand and had to think fast. I ripped it off and tossed it into the corner. This move made Maria suspicious of me, though I told her to stay.

She made her way into the warehouse of the art gallery and eventually got caught by one of Susie's goons. It was over the next thirty-six hours that I learned what the real purpose of Requiem was. Susie designed it as a multipurpose drug. In lower doses, it can be used by doctors to treat pain; higher doses it will get people unbelievably high, and both uses are available in pill form. Her favorite method, though, was a high dose in liquid form to be injected into someone's bloodstream directly.

It became a truth serum on steroids, a drug that would force you to speak on any subject, any terms. It didn't matter how hard you fought. The drug would put you into a sleep-like trance coaxing you into freely answering anything asked of you. The downside is that the high concentration of the drug would damage your brain and your heart. It was brutal on the body; it would turn you into a truth-telling corpse. The final design element was the burn rate; it would course through the system and metabolize so fast that it was almost impossible to test for. Unless someone was high and had recently taken the drug, you couldn't find it on any screen.

To scare everyone in the room, when Maria refused to cooperate with the interrogation, Susie showed us a multitude of videos on a laptop: The test subjects she used in South America to perfect the drug, showing us how quickly they deteriorated. They died, but not before they spilled every detail on whatever they were asked.

When Maria wouldn't talk, Susie decided to take her back to the house in the mountains where she had the drugs stockpiled. When they started loading up, I tried to make a move and go after them, shooting through two guards and taking heavy fire, but I was left behind as the plane took off the runway in Albuquerque. I tracked them back to Santa Fe and the house in the mountains where I found Maria, drugged up and a mess.

Susie had sped up the process and injected Maria on the plane. I could already see her deteriorating. That's when Maria and I had the worst conversation I've ever experienced. Those words will haunt me forever. I feel I will only get relief when I'm finally laid to rest, six feet under.

"Maria, I need to get you out of here. Did Susie shoot you up on the plane?" I could see her arm was bleeding.

"Yes, Erin, there's no going back. This is the end for me. You saw those same videos I did." She was crying.

"We can figure this out, get you to a doctor. Don't talk like this. It isn't over." I started crying with her.

"Erin, you know what you have to do. I'm already dying. I can feel my insides on fire. I can feel it working through me. It hurts, it hurts so bad.

You need to end this, protect Neil and the others."

"I can't do that to you. What you're asking of me, it's impossible to live with."

"Sometimes you need to step up. This is about the bigger picture. I can't have another psycho with leverage on Neil. He won't survive another run at it."

"Maria, this is going to crush him. Especially if he finds out it was me, I'm done for."

"They're almost back. You need to do it now before they get to you and do this. Please."

I stood in front of her, put the gun to her head, closed my eyes, and began to cry. I couldn't do it. I couldn't pull the trigger. That's when Maria lifted her hands up, put them on mine, held my hand over the gun, and pressed my finger. I knew it was over. I had no other choice. With tears running down both of our faces, we took one last big breath together, and I pulled the trigger. I took off running, tears blinding me, covered in the blood of the last person to ever trust me. It was the end of my world as I knew it; there was no turning back. At least that's what I thought at the time.

Before I've finished the story with Christian, he realizes how hard it was. We get up and walk out, talking and heading back to his place. It's close and a quiet spot to continue the conversation. It's after midnight when we get inside the small condo in the French Quarter. I sit down on his couch, fighting back the tears and telling him the rest of the story. He tells me I can stop, as he sees how painful it is for me to tell it. I've never shared the details with anyone before today.

"Marie, why didn't you tell Neil this? Why didn't you tell anyone? This isn't something you need to carry alone."

"Christian, it's my burden to carry. It's for me to deal with, to do what I can to try to make up for it by changing people's lives for the better." I can't stop crying.

"Neil should know. This changes a lot of things, even with the CIA. Do they know?"

You could see the emotion in Christian's face, even though he was trying to hold it back. As the tears continue to run down my face and my breathing continues to chase from my chest, Christian tries to soothe me as best he can. He's used to saving the day, but this is one day that I can never be saved from. It's harder to focus with each passing gasp. Though he tries to calm me, I find myself fighting for each moment.

"No, no one knows the truth. I think I couldn't come to terms with it until it started to eat at me. Promise me you won't tell Neil."

"If that's what you want, I promise. Can I ask you one last thing?"

"At this point, I'm an open book."

"Did you pick the name Marie because of Maria?"

"Yes; she was the last person to ever trust me. She did it without condition, and I wanted to be reminded of that forever."

"No one should ever carry that burden, Marie. You look exhausted. Are you going to be okay?"

"Can I stay here tonight?"

"Of course, let me get the room ready for you. I'll sleep on the couch."

11

"What was that chase all about the other night?"

I wake up in Christian's bed, fully clothed, just without my shoes on. Shit, I'm going to have makeup all over his pillows; that's embarrassing. Between the crying and my eye makeup and foundation mixing with the humidity, I'm a mess. All I remember is telling him I was exhausted, then him leaving the room. I must have fallen asleep on the couch. I wonder how I made it to the bedroom and lost my shoes.

After I get up and clean this clown look off my face, I'll look for Christian. It doesn't sound like anyone is here, and it's still early. As I walk into the bathroom, I notice a small note written on the mirror in some sort of marker.

Went for coffee and donuts, be right back – 5:45.

He left the time he wrote it so I'd know; how considerate of him. Since it wipes off with ease, my guess is it was a dry-erase marker. As I finish cleaning my face, I hear the door open and shut. He must be back.

"Christian, is that you?"

"Yeah, I have coffee, donuts, and some croissants, in case you weren't feeling a huge boost of sugar this morning."

"I'm sorry for last night, Christian. But after a long day, a big drink and then an emotional ending, I was just spent. Did you carry me into the room?"

"Yeah. I didn't want to leave you on the couch. So I put you in there, took your shoes off and left you to sleep."

"You're too kind. Thank you, though. I'll need to be heading back to my place to charge my phone. Where is it, by the way? Did I leave it somewhere?"

"It's plugged in by the coffee machine in the kitchen. I know how much it can suck when you wake up to a dead phone. When I got up at four to go for a run, I charged your phone."

This guy is something else. He's a total sweetheart, he's sexy as hell, but he's also five years younger than me. He's like a puppy as far as I'm concerned. I'm usually a fan of the older, established gentleman who can help me find my way. Maybe that's why I'm attracted to him; for his age, he is a gentleman with a big heart. Then there's also the fact that he's a talented investigator; he's the whole package.

"Christian, you really went above and beyond. I appreciate it."

"After hearing your story, Marie, it was hard not to. I'm here to cover your six anyways, but I can only imagine the burden you're carrying. I know you don't want me to tell Neil, but you should. It can just be an email or letter. He should know the truth about the woman he cared for so much."

"I understand. I hope to get that courage someday. For now, I'm going to work on everything in front of me. That's how I'll try to make something positive out of this shit show. I am going to help Neil and you guys take down Gaines Chemical."

"I guess my question is, why New Orleans then? Why not Detroit?"

"When we were in Santa Fe and Susie torched her plane with all that evidence in it, they scrambled a jet for her out of New Orleans. When I did some digging, I found they have had lots of flights to and from New Orleans in the past couple of years."

"Does that mean you assumed we could handle Michigan while you work a different angle?"

"That and the fact that I want to help, but not be close to Neil right now. Not until I deal with all of the emotion from that day."

"I can understand that, plus we have more than enough people working leads up there. No one is down here except the two of us, which leaves it wide open. Since you're the one who has the perspective and more time in New Orleans, what do you see?"

"The biggest clues to work from are related to Andy and the relationship he has with the city and police department. That will get us some more leverage on his connections with Gaines Chemical and how he plans on using Requiem. I saw up close what it does to someone. I can't allow that drug to hit the streets. This is more than just a case. You know that."

"Well, let's start to divide and conquer then. I'll keep working the police department and City Hall. Why don't you spend some more time trying to find Gaines's center of operations out here?"

"I think it's time to go back and talk to Diego. He's the smart one of the group. I bet he knows more than he let on in the beginning. He's the brains of the operation. Though Andy takes the credit, he does all the work."

"I can see that; Andy doesn't seem like the mastermind type. He's a megalomaniac, but that's about the only thing he has going for him."

"I should get back to my place to clean up and start the day. I'll hit you up later today. Thanks again for last night."

"No problem, Marie. I'm sorry you had to go through all that."

I make my way out of his condo and walk up Dauphine until I get close to where I'm staying. The walk back has me thinking about a few different things, different angles, and possibilities. I keep drifting off the current case and begin going back to when I was with Maria in Santa Fe. Seeing those videos and watching her deteriorate was too much. Last night and today roll into one mess of a day.

Back at my apartment, I reach out to Charlie and Diego to see what could be done. LT had told me Charlie would get ahold of me today, but these guys operate like two stoners in high school. They think they're accomplishing a record amount of work, only to find out they spent the afternoon watching Netflix on the couch. I finally get a call back from Diego around dinnertime; with my patience running thin, it was finally something to move on.

"Hey Marie, what are you doing for dinner?"

"I hadn't thought that far ahead for the evening quite yet. What do you have in mind?"

"Meet me at Irene's in one hour, and dress to impress. We need to talk about some things."

I got dressed and made my way over to the restaurant to find Diego there and the place half-empty. It turns out he rented out half the restaurant for us to sit down quietly together without prying eyes or ears. I noticed halfway through dinner that he was trying to make a play on me. Though it was over the top and a bit arrogant for him to think he could throw shiny things at me to get me to cave, I followed him down this path. The other two guys were rough. They were brash last night. Diego has a bit of talent; he's also a bit older than I am, and he is handsome. I have been struggling for human connection on any level. Talking to Christian about Maria brought up those feelings again. It reminded me of the hole I'm constantly running away from. Maria was the first and only connection I've made in a long time.

Though I know it won't be real, I do know it will help me in this case. If I can get some semblance of relief from the anxiety and sadness I've been fighting and get further in the investigation, I'm going to take it. You or my parents might say, "At what cost, though?" My response is simple. I lost my soul the moment I pulled that trigger on Maria.

There is no going back on that, no bringing her to life.

I can use the shell of myself to gather information, to go on this journey with Diego, and infiltrate this organization. This is risky, but no fault lies with the CIA for putting me back in the field. They knew I wouldn't stop doing things most agents wouldn't in my position, and they've used it to their advantage.

When you have walked down the path, taken the lives I have, there's no more off-limits. However, I can hear Christian's voice in my head telling me to keep from falling in too deep, trying to remind me this too shall pass. I can overcome it; it may not be perfect, but I shouldn't lose all semblance of the woman I've been.

As dinner was winding down, and he noticed I was acting into him, he started to push a bit about the other night when he had LT track me down at the Westin. I wasn't happy about it, but I played back into it and opened up about my intentions with Andy all along. At least it's the story I'm giving him.

"What was that chase all about the other night?" he asked.

"Diego, I don't understand the question." I say while eating, not even looking up.

"You know exactly what I'm asking. When I

had LT track you down at the Westin. You were hiding. I know you and Andy have some weird thing going on. That's how we met in the first place. What was your whole reason for searching for him? You've always kept it a secret. The reason Andy, and I, for that matter, never really cared is that we saw a tool we could use. We even said we didn't know your intentions, but we didn't care. We used our channels to check every database around. And it's not like some international agency is going to send some off-book to infiltrate a street gang and a dirty councilman for some low-level shit. So what's that real story?" Damn, his imagination is closer than he realizes.

"No, I'm not that cool. I've traveled the country, been in and out of a few organizations, some good and some bad. I had heard stories of a guy making waves by the name Andy the Brat. So I figured I'd come look for myself. It was a little curiosity and trying to hide from other poor choices." The best lies are part truth.

"How bad is your past? Is the law coming for you?" Diego asks.

"That part of my life is dead. The person I used to be doesn't even exist anymore. As far as the world knows, she is dead. If you want to go down this road, I'll walk out that door." I began to slide back in the chair and stand up. It was a strong play, but one I had to make.

"No, sit down, Marie. We all have our demons. You haven't given us a reason not to trust you. But we need to build up to higher levels of trust. Especially if you are going to be next to me."

"This is just dinner, Diego. You have some big plans for the second date, don't you?"

He smiled. "I do have one last question about your past. It's important for building trust. Then I'll drop it. I promise." He looked serious.

"Ok, but I can't make any promises." I'm trying to show some vulnerability.

"Have you killed before? I ask because you show a level of reserve I've only seen in people that have. I've been in this world a long time, and I can sense it." He was looking right through me.

"I have more than I'd like to talk about. That part of my past, I don't want to revisit. If you are asking me to kill for you, I'll leave, and you'll never see me again." My heart was racing. I didn't think this would go this way.

"What if my life depended on you taking a life?" He smiled and leaned back.

"If we make it to date four or five, then we can talk. But this is just the first dinner." I smile.

"Fair enough."

The rest of the dinner is us talking about Andy and him giving small details about their relationship, which was as I guessed based on the things I saw. I had been around them enough times that I was able to build a profile. That, combined with some of the details on how they met, gave me a greater picture. He'd let it slip just a bit earlier that he and Andy looked at me as a tool. They thought of me as something to use and possibly throw away. All this time, you were probably thinking, *how is Marie getting away with this*? They were probably thinking of ways to try and pin the money theft on me. The way Diego was questioning me, and asking me specific questions tonight, about what I had found out and how I found it out, has me thinking Andy was trying to use me as a scapegoat. That would be pretty easy since I have the money, and I'm the one that stole it from the people that stole it.

"Okay, we've been talking in circles for hours. Let me sum this up before you ask me back to your place. Let's be honest, that's what's coming next."

He damn near blushes. "How do you know I'm going to ask you back to my place?"

"Andy was or is still going to try and use me as a scapegoat for this missing money problem. He thought if he had me research it enough, he could get my hands into enough of the cookie jar that he could pin it on me even though it was all after the fact, right?" I tilt my head.

"He's not Andy the Bright. He thinks everything he does is perfect. He can do no wrong."

"Shit, did LT know this was the plan the whole time?"

"The whole gang did. It was part of the show. That's why I wanted to bring you to dinner. I'm tired of dealing with him, and I am blown away by you. I want to keep you out of his crosshairs and on my side. What do you think? Wanna pick a fight with Andy?"

"I like the way you think." I lean in over the table and kiss him.

The rest of the night we'll leave to your imagination. It was what I needed. And judging by his smile, Diego needed it, too. Most of the night was Diego speaking of his dreams, things he wishes for his family, his community, and the people he's supporting. He wants so much more than a life of crime and the underworld. He sees it as a way to serve a purpose. It's sad to see a man trapped in a world he knows he can't escape. It reminds me of the place I find myself.

"Marie, there's one other thing. Andy is going to pressure you to do something big for us. Something to prove your worth."

"Shit, do I have to steal something?"

"I wish it were that easy." He had the look of

death on his face.

"Ok, what are you talking about?" Now I'm getting worried.

"Andy is going to want you to take care of someone for us."

"You mean kill someone for you?" He won't say the words.

"I didn't say that. I said he wants someone out of the equation."

"So you won't say it, he won't say it. But I have to do it, or I won't what? Be allowed to hang around anymore?"

"I can protect you. That's not the issue. But I am concerned that he might do something stupid." He is getting more anxious with each passing phrase.

"Like come after me? Kill me even?" It's not the first time I've had my life threatened, so I just smile. "I can take care of myself. I've been threatened more than I'd like to admit."

"Please listen to me. I like you, I'd like to keep you around. We need to find a way to work through this. He hasn't told me who, but I'm fairly certain it's tied to this missing girl."

Diego continues in detail about his fears with Andy, bouncing back and forth with the jobs he's been doing. He really is concerned for me. I'm not sure if he brought that up to me out of fear for me, or fear of losing me. I'm sure it's a little of both. I can't hate him for that, but now I have to figure out how to make the councilman I just met, whom I'm supposed to help, disappear. This should be fun. On one side of the coin, I'm supposed to kill the guy. On the other side, I need to save his daughter and make the bad guys pay. This should be easy. Right?

Over the next few days, I learn a lot about the inner workings of the operation. For example, Diego was using Andy as a front for the crew and creating the cover. He also showed me how Andy would be an easy fall guy when the pressure comes. Diego is smart, not just street smart but also intellectually stimulating. It was common for Diego and me to have conversations about the stock market, international politics, and everything else between. For a bad guy, he was well-versed in many things. It made all the grunt work a bit more exciting and fulfilling. It doesn't hurt that he looks like a cousin of Antonio Banderas, along with that rasp in his voice. Mix in some salt-and-pepper hair and the physique of someone constantly training and you have Diego.

Diego did graduate from Tulane, as LT put it so quaintly. What he failed to mention is that he had a double major in biological engineering and business management. He never planned on a life of crime, but on a fateful night that changed his life forever, he was drawn into this world. The summer after he graduated from Tulane, before he was going to work on his master's degree, he was at a party with some friends. They weren't the cleanest of friends, but they were his childhood buddies. Growing up on the streets, you can't pick and choose who you're close to; you have to respect those that looked out for you even if they are now hustlers with rap sheets as long as this novel.

While he was at this party, someone ended up getting shot. That, mixed with the extreme volume of drugs present, resulted in his being charged with two others on conspiracy to commit murder, among other things. His family didn't come from money. He was at Tulane on a scholarship, which led to a poor defense and, ultimately, to him accepting a plea bargain for three years with parole. He figured if he were going to have a felony on his record forever, he might as well be the best damn criminal he could be.

Learning how Diego was brought into this world has given me perspective. It has also shown me how he sees Andy for what he is, a true rat. Diego may do the dirty work, but he follows a code. Not Andy; the only thing he follows is the code of look out for number one. Diego and I have talked plenty on the role Andy plays and what I'm doing here. The thing I'm worried about is that he keeps alluding to something but not saying it. I feel like Andy is coming after me, and hard. He just isn't telling me.

But that was for another time. It had been a long night, and I was trying to be in the moment, so I rolled back over into his arms and fell asleep.

12

"Well, that's a new wrinkle."

The past week or so has been crazy, just like Diego had expected. I have only been back to my apartment to check on things once. Since then, I have spent every waking moment with Diego and his crew, trying to formulate a way out in case things keep up. I have been ordering coffee delivery to me every day at the same time, from the same place. This way, if Christian needs to get me a message he doesn't want to send on my cell, he has a way of doing it.

Diego has been stressing out about Andy, his erratic behavior and this missing girl situation. I know he isn't telling me all that he knows, but he will in due time. I don't mean that as Marie the spy, but Marie, the concerned friend of Diego. I'm starting to blur the lines with him. Though it's been a short time, we both know we lie for a living, and there is some honesty in that. In certain moments, it's natural and can't be hidden. The quiet of the morning, the peace of the night. It's those simple times that keep us coming back for more.

We even spent three days at a beat-up storage facility going through everything imaginable out in the middle of nowhere, barely protected, with everything their operation needs, just sitting there under a simple padlock. The people in the area know what crew uses it, and they don't dare touch it. Same with the cops; there are so many fake names used to pay for the units that, even if they closed it, all they would do is start a war. Make the gangs work harder to increase their foothold. Why stir up a hornet's nest and risk collateral damage if you don't need to? It felt like doing inventory in a warehouse for some home supply store.

The real odd part was watching a few of the guys going back and forth toward a house off in the distance. It was a few miles out, but it was situated in a way you could tell it was out there; barely, but still. I had asked Diego about it, but he brushed it off, saying it was some place Andy kept, and to leave it alone. He really shot me down the two times I tried to ask about it. I put a mental note in there to come back later as soon as I had a chance.

As for the Andy situation dropped on my plate last week at dinner, that hasn't gotten any easier. Andy wants me to kill Wes, but he wants it to look like an accident. He thinks I'm some professional killer all of a sudden. I went from the cute girl on the outside to a useful killing tool. Either they know more about me than they are letting on, or they are so desperate to get this case behind them that they are willing to throw anything at anyone. When I say they, I mean Andy and his inner circle, which has a new member. There has been a small Asian girl that no one seems to know. Andy and Diego said she has a connection to a big client. Diego's let it slip a few times that the money I stole (he's still unaware of my involvement) was to go to Gaines Chemical for Requiem.

"Marie, Andy is coming over today. We have a meeting to go over what to do with Gaines. They're expecting a purchase from us. We are coming up short with the money and I can only do so much. Andy is looking for a scapegoat. That's why he wants you to make the father disappear. He's going to make the city think he took the money, as well as Gaines."

"Good morning to you, too." Playing the role of lazy supportive girlfriend for the day, I was still lying in bed.

"I'm serious. Do you have any ideas on how you can pull this off? You said you think you can make him disappear without killing him." I might have said that.

"I was just throwing out ideas. I'm assuming that stays between us? I shouldn't tell Andy that?"

"Hell no, Marie. He's crazy. He only cares about himself. He will throw you and me under the bus in one minute." Just then, one of Diego's men stuck his head in the room.

"Sir, he's here."

Diego kissed me and stood up. "We need to get moving." He pulled me out of bed.

"Give me fifteen minutes. I'll be ready. I promise."

Ok, so it took me twenty minutes, but I looked good. I was rocking black leather pants, a tight tee and a jacket. I walked down the hall like I owned the place. Even though it had only been a week, most of his crew had already warmed up to me. I had spent most of that time hanging out with them during the day and Diego at night. While he was off working, I helped them with everything they needed.

I worked with one of the younger girls on the crew on boosting cars and gave a few of them relationship advice. I taught two of his guys how to pick locks better. One might laugh, but Diego's crew is like family to him. I even got one of them to make amends with their mom. The best way to get a crew like that to respect you is to show them you will care for them. If you are going to be with the boss, you can't just be some superficial side piece and expect to get respect. You need to give them something, then you'll get it back. It might not have been a training montage for a fight scene, but it was worthy of a decent cut scene at least.

"She finally graces us with her presence."

"Hello, sir. Very kind of you to join us today." I gave him a hug and kiss on the cheek.

"You remember our associate? She'll be sitting in on this meeting to see if we are on pace with our end of the agreement. Which reminds me, have you been able to solve the problem we spoke of? I need that fixed by tomorrow night." Wait, for what? Here is Pan, always showing up, like one of those prickly things that get stuck in your shoe when you go hiking.

"Well, that's a new wrinkle. I guess I can turn up the timeline. I'm going to have to disappear for a while then." I looked at Diego.

"What do you mean?" Diego wasn't happy.

"The less everyone knows, the better. I'm going to get some things together. I'll get ahold of you when I complete my assignment." I quickly left the room, with Diego chasing after me. He got to me as I was almost back at the bedroom.

"Marie! Wait! Where are you going?"

"I have to figure this out. I can't do that here. The less you and everyone knows, the better." I leaned in and kissed him.

"Wait, where are you going? How are…."

"Don't worry, Diego. This has been amazing. I won't forget this."

"Are you leaving forever? What does that mean?" I have no idea.

"I don't know how long it's gonna take. I'm doing my best here." I kissed him again, this time really long.

"Marie!" I turned around and headed out as he called after me.

I quickly took off towards my place. Though it had been over a week, Christian and I hadn't talked. I know he's going to be livid. I had left my cell at the apartment when I went back, not wanting to risk him or Uncle Phil blowing my cover. I know he could have reached out to Uncle Phil and gotten notes on what to look for when working with me, but I wasn't about to throw a case away on the timing of a great connection.

He had been able to get me a few small details through my coffee order, though, so I was able to keep tabs on what he found; I just couldn't get any information back to them. It was a one-way street with very small pieces of information. It was just this morning that he had said we needed to meet up; the timing worked out well, with Andy putting the pressure on me. I had to get out and get a plan in place. I couldn't do any of this with Diego and his team around.

I finally made it back home, with an escort close by. Diego's guys think they know how to tail, but they aren't that good. I'm used to CIA and espionage tails. They are good enough for local shit, but not this. I was okay with them following me back to the apartment to sell the story, but I was going to have to leave them here.

13

"Sadly, I don't think Christian was recording it."

I had to get moving so I could head over to Christian's. Diego will ask, but I'll come up with something; I always do. I quickly moved through and out the back. Down a few houses and over some fences, and I was at the end of the block. I looked to ensure that no one was around and crossed the road, where I began to hurdle fences and make my way down some side streets. This was going to put me a bit out of the way, but it was better than getting caught. Christian and I need to sit down and review the past couple of weeks and see where the case stands.

In hindsight, I shouldn't have been as surprised as I was. Christian has people to answer to that aren't me. BCI and the FBI are utilizing him. I guess as I made my way up the fire escape to the back window, I should have reacted better when I saw him.

"Neil, what the hell are you doing here?" That was maybe too much attitude.

"Well, nice to see you, Erin . . . I mean Marie." Neil was calm. I wasn't.

"Christian, what the hell is he doing here?"

"He's following a lead and checking on the case. Had you checked your messages more, you would have seen I told you he was coming down. It's been almost two weeks. I got worried about you. It's not like I could fit it on the bottom of a coffee cup." Christian rolled his eyes at me.

"So what is he down here for? Support to check up on me? Give me a lecture?" I locked eyes with him.

"Marie, you need to calm down. If you'd like, we can get you a drink. No one is here to check up on you. Christian was simply concerned, wanted some help, and I wanted to follow up on a lead with Gaines and his operation down here personally. Is that okay, or is New Orleans off-limits to me?" Neil could feel the tension.

"You know that's not what I meant, Neil. It's just that after . . ." Seeing him got me worked up.

"You can be mad, or you can take it properly, but I'm already aware of most of it. Christian was

178

so concerned about you; he told me enough for me to ask you personally. Marie, this isn't a burden for you to carry alone."

I sat down on the couch and began to cry again. Whenever I think about that day, I just can't control it. I keep faking it to the world, and to myself, that I'm okay, and I will be fine. It's evident that isn't the case. Neil came up to me and put his arm around me. As I told him the story, you could see his emotions rise inside.

A man of his stature, known for being cool under the craziest of circumstances, was in the same place I was. I kept saying to myself that if he can deal with this and work with me to overcome it, then I need to stop looking at this as being weak. It didn't hurt that he told me just that as I was talking to him and revisiting the whole Maria incident.

"Neil, that's it. That's all of it. I don't know how many more times I can talk about it."

"Marie, because of that information, I have the FBI getting a warrant for Susie's personal effects that were logged when she went into prison. It's a long shot, but maybe we can get those videos off her phone. It will help us paint a picture of what Requiem does, what the drug is truly designed for."

The three of us just sat there, feeling the weight

of it all. The information and Neil's response to it made Christian and me a bit uncomfortable. It's not every day you have to tell someone you shot the love of their life, point blank, out of mercy. It's also not common for an employee to see their idol or mentor so vulnerable. It was an awkward twenty minutes that eventually became lighter when Neil was composed enough to try to comfort me.

"Neil, I get it. I need to work through this and learn to share the burden. But I took this on by myself. There was no one else there."

"That's where you are wrong. You share this burden with Maria. She was there with you. She knew what was going to happen and what needed to be done. The difference is that her burden was laid to rest when she passed away. Yours lingers."

"Well, maybe it will help you to know I'm going to help a bit down here. I can't hold judgment against you. I have to trust what your actions show me moving forward."

"Well then, let's start with all the shit I've been able to pull together from the past two weeks. Christian, do you have that map of New Orleans I asked you for?"

"It's on the table over there. What are we looking for?"

I walked over to the table and started comparing

my notes to the map, circling areas I've been to and others I have only heard about. My time with Diego brought me major insight into the inner workings of his operation, as well as Gaines's foothold in New Orleans. Since it's a port city, both guys use it to move products in and out. Susie, before she was arrested, would ship crates from Argentina to New Orleans. We aren't positive if the same number of products are still being moved in that fashion.

Neil and Christian will look into that while I continue to work my angle with Diego and his crew. Though I have to sacrifice some parts of myself, I know I'm getting some things out of it. I get intel for the case, but I also have someone that has shown they care about me. I could honestly see us together if I weren't a spy and he wasn't a crime boss.

"Okay, Marie, as you pointed out, we now have a lot of ground to cover. We don't want to get in your way, but we need all hands on deck. I'll reach out to our FBI contacts and try to get access to some undercover agents along with low-level surveillance to start building a case. Do you think you can help, or do we have to keep it hush-hush?" Neil was pressing me.

"I'll do my best. It all depends on how the next day and a half go. Diego claims that I'm free for the next couple of days. We'll see if he has a tail on me. Christian, think you can help me verify that in an hour or so after I get back to my place?"

"I got you. I'm also sorry about bringing in Neil on this, but I feel like I didn't have a choice." Christian looked like a sad puppy.

"I know you were just trying to do what was right. You were concerned about me and wanted him to know why. I can appreciate that. Plus if Neil can act this way, I can return the same kindness."

Neil took that as the perfect opportunity to check on what Christian had.

Christian started in on the contacts he had made and the information TJ and the FBI dug up from the police chief's office and staff. It looks as though one of his underlings is using their space to operate and move the cargo. From checking financial records and a few days of tailing, they've learned that it's not the police chief himself; they are reasonably sure it's a female officer named Lucinda Gonzales.

Christian's info suggested Gonzales was ruthless and surgical. I had already reached out to Jim Hammond, my old journalist friend, but he hasn't responded yet. It's not surprising, considering the way I left things with him. I know I didn't put him in harm's way or legal trouble with the story, but trust is hard to get back when you break it. I've been on a streak of blowing up relationships with anyone and everyone in my life. I guess that's why Neil being here and working the case surprised me.

Going back and forth, the three of us put together a game plan for how we would study Lucinda more, as well as her impact on Gaines Chemical. From the looks of her finances, one of their slush funds has paid her money. If she's working for or with Diego and Andy, perhaps it's simply as a liaison to Gaines.

"Well, boys, I need to get going, but I think we have plenty to look into and cover over the next couple of days. Christian, do we know how long Lucinda has been around the police chief's office?"

"We are looking into it as we speak. When I know more, you will too. I would assume she's a plant there. We need to find what leverage they're using on the chief, as well as track down the missing girl."

There's also a good chance there is nothing here. We could be chasing an empty lead. It happens a lot. We have some info on Lucinda, but it could also be Gaines's crew laying crumbs, keeping us and the Feds off the trail that we should be looking at.

"Slight problem: I have to figure out how to make the girl's father disappear." I headed toward the window I had climbed in.

"Wait a minute. What the . . . " Christian put his hand on Neil's shoulder. "Let me rephrase. When were you gonna bring this little nugget up?" Neil wasn't amused.

"She's used to working solo. Give her a minute. Neil, you're also famous for dropping shit on our plate. Maybe not quite like this, and you have a better track record. I'm just saying calm down." Is he defending me?

"Honestly, they just dropped this on my plate today. Well, sort of. I knew Andy might want me to do this, but he hasn't had the balls to ask me. Today, he brought it up in front of Gaines's liaison."

"Okay, let me get this straight. Gaines has a liaison with Andy, you have to kill this other councilman, and you have no plan for any of it?"

"That about sums it up, Neil. Half joking, I usually end up doing something that has a 50/50 shot of killing me. I'm hoping to have it all figured out before the end of the day or be dead, so it won't matter."

"We can't figure this out in five minutes. We need a plan to at least get him off the grid. Get out of here Marie. Let's plan on connecting tonight." Christian was still in protector mode.

"He's right. Now it's time to get out there and

turn over a few mattresses and see what turns up."
Neil had a shit-eating grin on his face. He was
proud of that one.

"Sounds good. Christian, let's keep messaging
through Snapchat; it will be the safest way for us
to stay in contact. Plus, Diego hates social media,
so he won't bother checking there. Not to mention,
I don't think he understands anything other than
Facebook or Myspace."

I'm not sure why I didn't think of it sooner.
Then again, I'm used to going at things solo. I have
to work on this team approach—it will probably
keep me alive longer. Not just with Neil and
Christian, but with Diego and his crew too. It's a
foreign feeling to me, on all fronts.

"Will do. Be safe getting out of here."

"Marie, we need you on this case. It's going to
take a team effort to get these assholes."

"I know. I'll do what I can."

As I climbed out of the window and down the
fire escape, I smiled at them and took off running.
I was always a fan of parkour, even went through
a bit of a phase in college. With my dad pushing
me to excel in so many physical challenges, I fell in
love with it. The free-moving and flowing ability
to traverse obstacles with ease drew me in. It's
gotten me out of jams in the past, that's for sure.

I'd be lying if I didn't say I felt a bit like a

woman scorned with Christian betraying my confidence and telling Neil about Maria. Then again, I stopped talking to him, hooked up with a crime boss, and looked lost. He was just trying to be a good friend and protect me. I can't get too upset. Also, the way Neil handled it makes me feel even worse. He's been more than understanding and caring, considering the situation. I mean, I took an amazing woman away from him. I know he's trying to show me that Maria was there too. There was also the Susie Gaines factor. I can't carry all of this on my shoulders, but it's hard to let go.

There were too many things distracting me, though. I had to figure out how to make Rivers disappear until I could save his daughter, get the money back to the city and frame Schwartz for what he actually did and clean up this whole mess. Step one is getting a plan in place, making it look like Councilman Rivers is gone. Luckily, Andy isn't that bright, so it's just about getting enough plausible connections through the media to sell the story.

Working my way across town, ducking into and out of alleys and over fences, I was able to get back in fewer than ten minutes. I kept checking to see if I was getting tailed, but it looks as though I made it free and clear. Back at my apartment, I sorted through my thoughts and worked through the information Christian gave me about the police chief and the contact at the city. This will be something I press Diego on, but I need to do it delicately.

It's getting late, I'm getting hungry, and I need to find somewhere noisy to go through my notes. Maybe I'll just walk down to Bamboula's and grab some takeout. I only have a few beers, some water bottles, and pretzels around here. I need something of substance. I called ahead and ordered the Cuban sandwich; it sounded good, and it's not a ladylike thing to eat. It's the perfect late-night food with fries. I can wash it down with some water or a light beer. They're essentially the same thing. At least that's how I look at it. One just has some carbs and a relaxing effect to it. I shot Christian a text to have him head this way to see if I have a tail.

I waited a bit too long to head down there, but this did give Christian time to get over here. It's been almost thirty minutes since I ordered the food. Still, I was distracted with this case tree I've created; the new information given to me by Christian has my mind working. I was trying to go through the people I had met or heard about during my time with Diego. I then tried connecting them back to the foundation Christian and I are building. I was tying my shoes when I saw a text from Christian saying he's outside.

As I walked out the front door and made my way down Frenchman, I put my head down, and my hat even lower. I used windows, car mirrors, and anything with a reflection to keep an eye on my peripherals. I knew I had Christian somewhere over my shoulder, keeping an eye on me, so I didn't have to give it away. I was looking at my phone, waiting for his text, but I hadn't received anything yet when I walked into the bar. Bamboula's is a big small bar; in New Orleans that makes perfect sense. Bars out here aren't about size, but quality and atmosphere. This place had plenty, with TVs all over the walls and a bar that runs the length of almost the whole restaurant, with that old New Orleans vibe in the woodwork around the brick and in the ceiling.

"Hey miss, what can I get for you?" the bartender asked.

"I'm here for a pickup order. Under Marie."

"One Cubano? They actually messed it up, not sure how, but they're making a new one. Care for a drink while you wait, on the house?" What a gentleman.

"Sure, I'll just take a Stella bottle."

I'm not a beer fan. I drink it because of that fact. It keeps me measured, allows me to have a drink or two and stop. This place is hopping for a late dinner crowd, and the vibe is strong for a Sunday.

While sitting there, lost in my phone and my notes, I saw a message come through from Christian. "Pretty sure the black Honda CRV was tailing you. I'll know for sure when you head back." I was halfway through my beer when my food came out. I paid and went on my way.

I started the walk back with my food in hand, hat over my eyes, and at a decent pace. It makes it easier to spot them if you change pace and direction. I shot Christian a text, letting him know I was diving down the alley before my place to see how these guys react. As I quickly sidestepped and sprinted down the path, I made my way into a neighbor's yard with a quick move, almost YouTube-worthy. Sadly, I don't think Christian was recording it.

Finally, back in my apartment with the tail shaken, I was waiting to hear from Christian about what he's seeing. While leaning on the kitchen counter with my food container open and fries in my mouth, he called.

"Hey Marie, I'm certain these guys were tailing you. I'll text you the car and plate info so you can keep an eye out in the future. After you made that move, they circled the block two times before they gave up."

"I guess that's pretty obvious then. I'll know for sure if Diego texts or calls. . . . Look at that, right on time. I'll call you right back."

It's almost sad that he called this quickly. It means he doesn't trust me. I have given him no reason not to. That does not mean there aren't plenty of reasons not to trust me in their own right, or to realize I'm a wolf in sheep's clothing among the herd.

"Hey Marie, how's your night going?" Diego is playing nice.

"It was going okay, but I'm pretty sure I was being followed by some shady-looking guys. I had to ditch them. I wasn't sure if it was friendly or not."

"Those would be my guys checking up on you. I just want to make sure you are safe. There are a lot of people that want to see me harmed, even if that means going after someone like you."

"Well, I guess we're going to have a problem then. You either trust me or you don't. Regardless of the reason, you're putting a tail on a woman you're hanging with without her permission. Come on, you know that's pretty shady."

"Okay, you've got me there. If I had a little sister and some guy did that to her, I'd be pissed."

"Maybe we can come up with a happy medium, because if I catch another tail and it's one of your goons, we can call this a friendship and stop now. Which is sad, because I like you."

"I like you too, Marie. If that's the way you want it, I have to respect it. You've shown you can protect yourself; I need to trust you, especially with Andy and now Gaines's guys on the prowl. This request on Rivers has me worried." I could hear Diego's voice crack.

"Tell you what. I'll text you more often, just to let you know I'm good. Will that do? Will that be good enough? I can handle Andy, just like I got rid of your team." I was still hot.

"I can live with that. Thanks for understanding. I care about you. Though it's been a short time, I don't want to see any harm come to you."

"Have a good night, Diego. I've got some work to catch up on."

"You know, you're still pretty secretive about your work."

"You can't really talk. You've told me some, but not all." And this is how I get him.

"Okay, that's also a great point. I'm losing a lot tonight."

"You'll lose a lot with me in general."

"Okay, Marie, I'll let you have a great night. If I share more with you in the coming days, will you reciprocate?"

"It would be the honorable thing to do." To make some shit up.

"Good night, girl."

"Night, Diego."

Like that, I was off the phone, but feeling a little dirty. I like him, but I know he's just part of the job. It's hard not to judge myself for what I'm doing and how it affects me. Since Santa Fe, I've lost a part of myself, but talking to Neil has opened the wound back up. In a good way, though; I feel it's ready to heal, and not just scar over.

The call with Christian was a quick one. We went over the tail and what Diego claimed to be true. We agreed that I would lay low until Christian can get back over here in the morning. That way, we can check one last time to see if Diego is keeping his word. For the rest of the night, I'm going to pick at my food, review all these notes, and add onto my tree.

14

"I doubled back to my car and made my way toward the house."

C ases can often take days, weeks, or even years to come to a conclusion. You're probably familiar with the amount of time it took Neil to catch Cappelano. It's not for lack of effort. As an investigator, you can't go crashing in and announcing your presence, or the bad guys change their routine and make it even harder. This is about finding patterns. Last night I stayed up late, even fell asleep on the couch; my sleeping patterns are getting worse. I made sure to text Diego to wish him a great day to see if I can keep his guys off my ass.

Today I want to spend time doing some recon on the plants, warehouses, and connected spots

Christian and I came up with. I can't do it in my Jeep; that'll be too obvious. For now, I'm going to work with Christian to ensure I can ditch a tail, then have him drop me off at Harrah's Casino. I shot him a text, and he quickly replied, saying he was almost in place.

I had a lot of ground to cover, so I had to get off the grid. I needed to take Councilman Rivers off the game board and convince Andy that he's dead, while preventing his daughter from thinking that. I need to move some pieces around, and I only have an afternoon to do it. Luckily, I have help from Christian and dare I say it, Neil. I'm not a fan of help, but having those guys around is like a cheat code.

Thanks to the car rental app Turo, I snagged a car no one would notice me in. I also got to enjoy the ride a little bit. A Mustang, with a top and everything, unlike my Jeep, and all the conveniences I might need for driving around town and hiding in plain sight today. The best part about it is the car's windows are tinted so dark no one can see in it. After I was up and ready, morning pills (yes, my Flintstones) in hand and running out the door, I began walking toward the center of the French Quarter to see if I had a tail.

With a similar routine as the night before, hat down and good gait, I looked at my phone. It just looked like I was scrolling through social media. I even took a few selfies to use the camera and look behind me. Yesterday, the guys were in a Honda CRV, which I don't see. That doesn't mean they aren't on foot or in a different car. As I turned down Decatur to head toward the casino, I noticed two guys fall back quickly. Then, a car up ahead did a fast U-turn.

These guys still believe I'm an amateur. This should be fun. I can't wait to make them scramble again. Christian texted me, confirming the very same thing I was thinking. I told him to meet me at the parking lot where he was staying. This would give me time to ditch the tail, lose them in the city, and get a ride from Christian to my rental.

Headphones on, blasting some Jon Bellion, backpack tucked tight, I started to increase my speed a bit to a light jog. As the beat started to pick up, I ducked down a side street, then over a fence into a blocked-off courtyard. I could feel the rhythm pushing me, matching the adrenaline and pumping of my heart. I found my way down another block, then into another courtyard. With the songs increasing in speed, I began taking risks, pushing it over obstacles. At this point, I had already lost the tail; now I was just having fun. Over fences, through small openings and in and out of courtyards until I found myself sliding into the garage at Christian's hotel.

It took me a good thirty minutes from the time I started my run to the moment I slowed down in the dark, damp garage. I slowly pulled my headphones back and slid into his car, and we took off toward the casino, where he parked and dropped me off at the hotel across the street that's connected to Harrah's. As I made my way down the escalators and through the tunnel, I noticed I was free and clear. Not many people are around this time of the morning, and I could finally relax a bit. I slowed my pace and messaged the person for the car through the app, telling them I was a few minutes behind.

After a quick and easy check-in process and a short conversation with Christian, I was on my way. We had an idea on how to make Wes disappear, but I had to get a message to Diego and get him to convince Andy not to tell the daughter to keep her calm. I don't want her to have to go through the extra grief of thinking her father is dead, on top of this extra shit Andy is putting her through. I shot Diego a quick message that I had an idea, but I needed assurances that Andy wasn't going to upset the girl with the news. He asked why, and I said, *Have a heart*. That shut him up pretty quick.

I headed toward the storage facility that Diego

had taken me to last week. It's not the same one we robbed, but it was one that he had me work in with him. This one looked like it was in a bad sci-fi movie. It's old and gray, hasn't been maintained in years, and is being strategically attacked by foliage on all sides. The importance of this shithole is its proximity to that house out here in the middle of nowhere. I remember noticing a few cars heading out in its general direction when working with Diego those couple of days.

The house is decent-sized, old and worn but with character. The property feels like it should be on a farm in the middle of Kansas. Instead, it's in the middle of a small forest of Louisiana trees, surviving in this heat and humidity. None of the neighbors within earshot realize the number of drugs that get moved into and out of here. Or they just don't care. It's amazing what we can get used to if our neighbors leave us alone.

Diego said his crew could supply the majority of Louisiana and a large chunk of East Texas, including Houston. *That* is what Gaines sees with New Orleans and the rest of Louisiana. It's about the international ports, access to states like Texas and cities like Houston. A new drug is just like any other product: You need to get influencers to like it, talk about it, and spread the word. Get them hopped up on it on vacation in the Big Easy, then watch them crave it back home.

Within a block of the storage unit, I parked the car in the street and started my way up on foot; armed only with my cell phone and backpack, I began looking around. I'm mainly here to do some recon. I don't expect to see anyone around, as Diego said they're rarely out here. People know not to mess with this place. This will give me the time I need to break into a few different storage containers that I'm certain belong to Diego and his crew.

There aren't any security cameras out here, plus no one has the fortitude to steal from these guys. Not to mention they don't want any footage of them getting involved in the shit they do. When you look at the area they're set up in, their influence over the locals and police, this is like a safe zone for them to operate. It's a little off the grid. Even cell coverage is spotty out here.

I worked my way around the complex, looking for signs of life. I wanted to make sure I could operate uninterrupted. I knew Christian wasn't far behind if I needed him, so once I knew it was clear, I began picking locks and working my way through. The first couple of units were nothing other than chemicals, some cash, and basically garage shit.

I was looking to see where they were hiding the

drugs. They had to be somewhere around here. Maybe they moved them to make room for the Requiem purchase they're hoping to bring in. From what I've learned from being a blonde on a wall, this is their routine: Keep the drug surplus here, then move it to the house up the street, where they load it into cars, containers, and trucks. From there, they move it out to all the places they'll sell it. Whether it's the streets of Houston or the French Quarter, it's a system that has made them mountains of money.

I shot Christian a text telling him where the next stop was so he could get a head start and scout it out for me. With my search coming up empty, I doubled back to my car and made my way toward the house. He parked up the street and started walking in as I did the same. We didn't want to get noticed, so it was a bit of a pain. It's par for the course.

Christian was coming from the southwestern corner, and I was approaching from the opposite side. He was looking in from the rear of the house, and I had a view of the front. It was your typical Colonial with a Louisiana flair, covered in green stuff. It looked as if it were a late '80s or '90s build. You may ask how I might know that; I had to play a real estate agent on a case a few years back. There was a decent amount of activity for this early with no cars or trucks to be loaded.

Between Christian and me, with a few texts, we counted about a dozen people working the grounds. There was some commotion in the upstairs bedroom, but the curtains were closed. I say commotion, but it was just a lot of shadows or bodies moving in and out. I tried to move for a better look when I saw someone pull the curtains back and open a window for some cool air. Wait a minute—is that the missing girl? I shot Christian a text—*Hey, do you have a picture of that girl on your phone?* He quickly texted one back.

Holy shit, that *is* the missing girl. I swear it is. She even has the same shirt on from the picture. Luckily, on social media, teens often post way too many pictures. That means we have a picture of the last thing she was seen in. These goons still have her in the same clothes. I fight the urge to risk it all and run in there.

If I didn't think that it would probably put her in harm's way, I'd go in right now. She isn't old enough or trained to handle the kind of trauma that can come from a shoot-out. I also just don't think it's right. Since Christian doesn't have much of an angle, he started to make his way toward me. After a few short minutes, he was up on top of me, whispering into my ear.

"That's her, all right. I can see her plain as day."

Christian was using his camera's zoom.

"I thought that was her. I knew it was implied that they tied Diego up with Andy in this against his will, but so close to home? Diego made it sound like Andy was off on his own. Doesn't this look like Diego knows more than he's letting on?" Shit. I know we aren't truthful, but damn.

"I'm used to long-ass stakeouts. Neil is still in town. I suggest I sit here and keep an eye in case she is moved. Other than that, there's not much we can do. Marie, did you really think Diego wasn't involved in this part?"

"I truly did. There weren't any signs of it. And he and Andy are more reluctant partners than best friends in the business. It's like watching a musical group gripe off stage, then play on it. I'm still holding out hope." Barely, I might add.

"Sounds like it; you'll have to push Diego's buttons to try to get some information out of him. I'll let Neil know what I found. We're gonna have to speed up the process on Wes." Christian was right.

"I guess I'm heading out to see what kind of moves I can make. I don't see Diego's car here. Then again, he told me this place is Andy's. When I pushed, he got angry. Maybe I can get his attention tonight. I'll call him from the road. Be safe, Christian; call me if anything changes."

"Will do. Stay safe. You're operating in murky waters."

Shit, I know I am; it's the life I lead daily. He's just like a good big brother. Since he can't be there to cover my six, he's trying to give the old *good luck*. This case is heading down the path we were expecting, but that doesn't make it any less dangerous. I need to get back to New Orleans and see if I can hang out with Diego tonight to find out what's going on, what his play is, and whether this is simply Andy messing around. He is aware Andy has me looking into the lost money, though he's been fine with me not working. He's been focused on time with me, as opposed to figuring it all out.

As I made my way across the lake again for another trip, I felt an idea forming. I need a way to pin most of this on Andy, since he's already primed to be a fall guy. Maybe I am falling for Diego, since I keep taking my focus off his role in all of this. With Christian tied up, I think I might need to call Neil and bounce some ideas off of him. For most of the stuff I want to do, Uncle Phil would simply report me to my overwatch group. It wouldn't end well; Neil is my only chance of pulling this off.

At this point we have a vested interest in Gaines Chemical and their destruction. We've both seen that the machine is so large it will be hard to bring down with a single blow. It's going to take a systematic approach to remove the limbs of his tree and work our way back to the base. With an organization woven together so tightly, going after the roots too early can simply create spin-off factions and new trees.

We need to handle this just right. We learned through Gaines's first imprisonment that it won't slow him down; it merely pissed off his sister and sped up the process. Off the bridge and exiting the freeway, I texted Diego to see if we could hang out, or if I could stay at his place. While waiting for a response, I worked up the courage to call Neil and ask him for help.

I looped him in on what we found out at the house and brainstormed what we needed to do next. For my part, I wanted to raid the house immediately, but I know there wasn't enough information to do so. There are so many investigations into Diego, Andy, and Gaines that it's not that simple. Neil said he was going to loop in the FBI and let them handle the decision with the locals. I was going to work on a plan on getting the girl out ASAP. That's the hard call people like Neil and I have to make. Weighing the risk of that girl over a case like Gaines that could kill thousands of girls like her. It's not that simple.

Off the phone with Neil, I took a deep breath. I

couldn't help but feel a sense of relief. It wasn't some life-altering thing, but it was like getting over the fear of jumping off a high dive. It was simply surviving the ordeal. The conversation had me in knots the whole time. I think I would've rather had to sit down with my parents in high school and inform them I was pregnant and dropping out of school. That's how scared I was to talk to him, but I pulled off the bandage and can now focus on this missing girl.

I walked back into my apartment and made my way into the shower to clean up in hopes of hanging with Diego. It was odd; I was finding myself anxious about his reply. Waiting and hoping were weighing on me more than normal. I know that my current mental state isn't where it usually is. Not sure it will ever go back since Santa Fe. I took a long, Neil Baggio-type of shower for a change, less about utility and more about release.

After nearly running out of hot water, I rinsed off and stepped out. While drying off, my drifting thoughts were interrupted by a knocking at the door. It was Diego. That's odd—why didn't he call? I'd say I need to get dressed first, but he's seen me naked more than once. I opened the door, with a big smile on, playing the fun-loving girlfriend.

"Hey Diego, what's going on? You didn't message or call me back. Is everything okay?" He looked half scared and half pissed.

"No, it's not. I think Andy double-crossed me, or pissed someone off."

"What's going on? Is someone after you? You have me scared." I am, but not why he thinks.

"Someone broke into our storage units across the lake. The problem is we don't have security cameras, and it's damn near public knowledge we store shit there. It's protected from reputation more than anything. Without that, we are just some two-bit hustlers, with no respect and no product. I need to send Andy a message; this stunt he pulled is affecting business."

"What are you talking about? I'm looking into that theft, but we both know he probably just spent it on something else. It looks like an inside job anyway. Like you were saying, he can't be trusted, he's just a shill for you to control. But now it's affecting business. Is there anything I can help with?"

"Marie, I don't think you understand. Without carefully removing him, we could lose all his cover, all the connections he has built. I'm not there yet. I need more time to cultivate those relationships. It's that damn girl. He had to pull that stunt. On top of everything Councilman . . . "

"Stop right there. We aren't talking about the other councilman. Some things in this relationship we just keep a secret."

"You're right. It's just like the girl. You know the one. We talk about it, but not really."

"Diego, what girl? Is Andy involved with the disappearance of that girl on the news?" No shit, he is.

"Yes, and he has me helping cover his tracks. I need to get her out of there ASAP, find a way to get her back home without anyone noticing. Unless you can help with that, I don't know what my next move is. I need time to think. I just don't know if I can afford to take it."

Let's be honest here. I know about the girl. He's kind of told me about the girl, but he's never come clean all the way. It's always been this implied bullshit. Honestly, the majority of our relationship is like that. That's the part that makes this feel almost real, more than normal. We are both openly being fake, and we are okay with it. We are so desperate to find something more than an empty night with someone that we'll settle for a fake relationship. The problem is that I think we are both catching real feelings for each other in the process.

"Is that why you came here? Same reason I reached out? Stressed and in need of some help?"

"Exactly, babe. When I talk to you, it helps me think. I haven't given you all the variables in the world I operate in, but I think I need to so that I can bounce some ideas off of you." Yes, please tell me more. Can I record it?

"I'm here for you. I just needed a distraction, and this is a huge one. I'm here for you in any way I can be."

"I guess I'll start at the beginning. How I met Andy and got involved in this shit in the first place."

Diego and Kevin Andrew Schwartz went to Tulane together; it was a party that Schwartz threw, but it wasn't in a poor neighborhood, as he made it out to be before. Schwartz's father was connected and got an excellent attorney who made the whole thing look like Diego and his friends bought all the drugs. Their friendship was torn for years because of it. Then one day when Diego, fresh out of prison, was struggling to find work, Schwartz approached him with an idea.

That's when the persona Andy the Brat came into the picture. It was a way to insulate Kevin and his friend Diego. They created an identity that could be played by almost anyone to create confusion while they worked the system. Though Diego was pissed, he knew it was a great business opportunity. With nothing else arriving at his doorstep any time soon, he took the offer. He vowed one day to return the favor to his old college buddy.

"Let me get this straight, with the way things are. Would you be open to me helping you put the screws to this guy? The only question is, are you even aware of the damage the new drugs Andy is trying to buy can do? It's brutal shit. It makes heroin look like child's play."

"That's not what Gaines said. He sells it like a solution to the world's drug problems. Aren't they selling that shit legally as Trustia, or some shit?!" Diego was getting visibly pissed.

"I'm going to call some friends from the dark web that don't want to be known. But they can get me some footage you need to see. I will also go to work on using those same people to make Andy the culprit for those missing funds."

"If you can help me do all of that, I think I would use a word I only use with my mother, as it pertains to women." He smiled, and almost blushed. It was cute.

"Oh, Diego, I've only known you a few weeks. I appreciate the sentiment, but I hate that guy as much as you. This will be just as much fun as anything else." Is he talking about the L-word?

It's moments like this that make me fall for him. It's the honest moments that show his true colors. He cares about his community. He knows his place, but he still has rules he follows. He's not going to push things to a different level. As we spoke, I started curling up in his arms. At this point, I just had my towel and a blanket on. I hadn't even moved to get changed.

The more I find myself catching real feelings inside, the more I outwardly act as if I don't. It's real high school childish shit, but it's a defense mechanism that goes way back. It's also one that has kept me alive, so I'll keep it going for a while.

Diego and I sat there talking about all the stress between him and Andy and how Diego had plans to get out from under him, but has to use his coverage to stay out of prison. At the end of the day, the name of the game is survival. I get it; you can't kill the golden goose that keeps you free, even if he is the reason you have a target on your head in the first place.

As we talked, I tried slipping in false truths that were based in reality, but altered slightly. I was trying to open up to him in my own way. We sat there for nearly an hour when I realized I had to get him out of there so I could call Neil and get things moving. He also had to get Andy going and figure out what was going on with the storage units. He was less mad about it after we spoke and chalked it up to turf war shit since he had a new target to focus on: Andy!

"Thank you, Marie. What do you need from

me?" Diego went from stressed to smiling.

"I need some privacy. How about I meet you back at your place in an hour or so? I'll call you when I'm heading that way."

"Sounds good."

Like that, Diego kissed me with the most passion I think I've ever felt in a kiss. Especially one from a man, but that's a different story. As he walked out, I checked my phone, realizing I never texted Neil about Diego; I didn't have time to. Luckily I didn't have any messages from him. I started dialing him right away, hoping he and Mike hadn't gotten to move on anything yet.

"Neil, it's Marie. We need to hold off the raid for at least twelve hours. Can you get me that much?"

"Do I even want to know why?"

"Probably not, but if they press you on why tell them I think I can get the girl back without anyone needing to use force."

"I hope you know what you're doing. This would be huge for us, for the case, and for this girl."

"I won't let you down, Neil. I've done enough of that for one lifetime. I do need a favor, though. I need TJ's help on something. I might be able to get Andy to be the fall guy for the money I stole on top of the kidnapping."

"I'll shoot TJ a message and tell him to get ahold of you."

As I got off the phone, I started to well up again. It reminded me of dealing with the loss of Maria at my own hands. The rest of the night and tomorrow are going to be about moving a lot of parts to bring this case home.

15

"With the rain masking any sound and the darkness allowing me to move freely around the house, I began searching…"

From the moment I got off the phone with Neil until TJ finally called me, I couldn't help but think about Santa Fe. I wanted to ensure I don't make any mistakes and put someone else in harm's way. That's my biggest concern with the girl, with a raid, and with what could happen. I don't think I could handle two preventable deaths in such a short period. I needed to do this right, needed to find a way to be the force of nature I felt I was before Santa Fe. TJ finally called, damn near giving me a heart attack, as I was deep in my own shit.

"Yo, Marie, it's TJ. Neil said you needed my

help. He also said we're trying to save a teenage girl. What do you need?" TJ was chipper.

"Thank you for your help, TJ. I need to find a way to wash the money I took from Andy, the stuff he stole from the city. We need to clean its trail, digitally at least, then move it back to Andy's accounts and put it back into the city's funds. They need that money, but he needs to go down."

"This isn't a movie. You know that, right? But I'll talk to my guy who specializes in this kind of stuff and see what I can come up with. Give me a few hours. What can I do for you with the girl?"

"The biggest thing I need is an point person at the house for her and her dad. When I deliver her to her father, I need a bit of cover, a covert way of doing it; think of it as a window of opportunity. I'm working on finding a way to pin that on Andy too, but I don't want to get some other contacts attached to it. I also need some intel on a few relationships."

"You got it. I'll get with Neil and Mike on that window you need. Just email me the background data you are looking for and I'll dig in."

"Thanks. Keep an eye out for the email. I'll send it as soon as I get off the phone."

"Good luck. Neil and everyone else knows you're in a shit spot. We've got your back."

"Thanks, TJ."

Shit, does everyone know what's going on? Does everyone know what I went through? I know it's for the best—that way people will have context—but part of me wanted to keep those horrors to a minimum. I looked outside to make sure Diego had left; I didn't want to risk getting walked in on while talking to TJ or Neil. It's going to be more efficient if I can call them together.

I just shot TJ a message having him put Neil, Mike from the FBI, and me on a conference call. That way I can go over this stuff in one quick shot. TJ messaged back, saying it would be a minute or two for him to get everyone on the same call, but he was on it. I took a minute to grab my tablet and review the new files I received on the missing girl from Christian and Neil's team.

Something still isn't sitting right with me. I don't feel as if the missing girl's father is truthful. Most of the men around me right now are less than honest. There is something off about Councilman Wes Rivers. I just don't know what it is it yet. Neil has him hidden, but even though he's off the board I feel something is going on there. It could be simply the fear of retaliation from his former partner-turned-crime boss. However, he's hiding more than he's letting on. As I began going down the rabbit hole of possibilities, TJ called.

"Hey TJ, did we get everyone?"

"Yeah, we have Mike and Neil on here along with the two of us."

"Okay, guys, let's keep this simple. I'm going to talk for a bit, tell you what's going on and what my idea is. Then you let me know if you're good with it."

After a few minutes of small talk and shit-talking, I was able to get control of the phone again. Neil and Mike have a tendency to rile each other up. I remember Maria talking about it. She used to tell me it was like hanging out with two college frat boys sometimes.

"Okay, now that we've got that over with, let's get down to it. Christian still has eyes on the girl; from last communication, she hasn't been moved. What I do know is that Diego is getting tired of his partner's antics. Councilman Schwartz, aka Andy the Brat, is acting erratically. I was able to convince Diego that I can be the driving force in bringing Schwartz down, getting the girl home, and keeping the cops out of it. He wants nothing to do with that girl and wants her home, as we all do, especially now that he thinks Councilman Rivers is missing or dead. He wants this over, and Andy off the board ASAP. If I can get a small window to deliver her without anyone seeing me, I can keep my cover and get you the girl. Does that work for you guys?"

"How much time do you need? I'm quite sure I

can give you a ten-minute changeover window to help sell it," Mike replied.

"Thanks, Mike. I appreciate that. TJ, were you able to come up with an idea on how to move the money around?"

"Neil actually has a great idea; I thought I'd let him share it," TJ directed us.

"Well, Marie, we have access to a large cover slush fund. It's as close to untraceable as you can imagine, and I think you're trying to do what's right here. We are going to use the money you took and funnel it back to an account we created in his name. It makes it look like he set up an offshore account in the Grand Cayman. We have a contact down there from a previous case helping us out."

"At this point, I trust you guys. I know I can't do this on my own, though I try. I'll get the info over to TJ so he can access the cash and move it around."

"Thanks, Marie. Just call me with it when we get off the phone so that there's no paper trail of any of this." TJ has a point.

"All right, guys. I'll do that then head over to Diego's and set up getting the girl home. Mike, I'll message Neil or TJ to confirm when I'm bringing her by."

"No need. Just text me directly; I'll have TJ send you my info. I'll take care of the rest."

"Thanks, Mike. I'll talk to you guys later."

I hung up, then immediately called back to BCI to talk to TJ and give him the information he needs to move the money around. It's going to be a rough one. It was nice having access to funds again, but I'm resourceful. I can always ask Diego to get me cash to make this problem go away as a way to build up money.

Off the phone and organized, I sent Diego a message letting him know I had good news and I'd be right over. It took me nearly twenty minutes to get over there, but listening to some music calmed my nerves. This case has me on edge, which isn't surprising. With the way the case in Santa Fe ended, I already had anxiety to spare. I can't lose another person, not like I did before. There is sometimes collateral damage; it's part of the job. But this was different.

As I walked into Diego's place, I noticed he didn't have anyone around. His normal driver was gone, his door guy was nowhere to be seen, and it seemed quiet. As if my anxiety isn't high enough already, I had to deal with this now. I was walking around an empty house, with no one in sight. His message said he was home, but there's no sign of him anywhere.

I called out, "Diego, are you here?" No response, just an eerie silence. I continued to walk around the house, then heard a creak in the floorboards. I was already looking over my shoulder on a constant pivot when I saw the shadow. I kept a steady pace, preparing myself to be attacked.

Then from around the corner, as anticipated, a man lunged at me, trying to grab my shoulders. I turned around, ducked, and sidestepped him. He was a large guy; he reminded me of a bigger version of my father. Lucky for me, my father taught me that speed and technique could overcome size and strength, especially when the fight has no rules; there is nothing saying I can't tee off on his crotch or throw something in his eyes.

He turned to face me, which is when I noticed it was the same guy that threw me off the ship a few weeks ago. I should say "attempted to," since he didn't completely clear the bottom deck. I didn't bother trying to wait for him to come back at me. I sidestepped him one more time, kicking his knee. He dropped down and fell back a bit, allowing me to gain leverage and throw a solid combo to his face.

I jumped on him, straddling his neck as I took him to the ground. That's when his eyes got bright and big, staring me down. You could see him running through the possibilities in his head of who I am. I put my hands around his neck and started to smash his head into the ground, trying to disorient him enough for me to put him in a chokehold.

"You crazy bitch! Andy knows it was you who stole the money. He knows you're working with Diego. Now you're both going to die."

"Andy doesn't know shit about anything! If he knows or thinks I did anything, give me one reason why I should believe you're not just making shit up to kill Diego and me?"

"We know you were on the boat. We recognized you."

"Did you ever find the money on me then?" I continued to hold him down, pressing his head into the ground.

"No, we didn't. Actually, we never had any connection." He was bleeding pretty good.

"No shit. This means Andy has nothing on me, cause I didn't do anything. He's just trying to get you two idiots to kill Diego and me. This is an easy way to flip you." Remember, I specialize in creating doubt.

I rolled off to the side and grabbed his arm while straddling my legs around his neck. I was starting to cut off his oxygen. As he fought and faded in and out, I was able to get some information out of him. They had sent him and his partner to get Diego and me and to take us back to

Andy. There's a chance the other guy and Diego are still around here somewhere. He kept fighting off the hold; I felt myself put more and more pressure on him until he stopped moving. I'm going to assume he's just taking a long nap and leave it at that.

I jumped up and began working through the house quickly, looking for any signs of Diego or someone else. They always work in pairs, rarely groups of threes or fours. This is lowly thug shit; they aren't ex-military. I can only assume it's one of the geniuses that was with the other guy on the boat. I didn't see any signs of him around the house, but then I realized they might already be in the car, waiting for the other guy to bring me out.

I doubled back out the door to the yard, working my way around the front of the house. It began to rain. When isn't it raining in New Orleans? The city was covering me with a blanket of night. With the rain masking any sound and the darkness allowing me to move freely around the house, I began searching for the partner to the man I had just incapacitated. I made my way around to the front, but still didn't see anything. This is where I noticed the van I had pulled up behind was running with the lights on, but there was no one in the front seats.

Looking inside, I didn't notice much. I moved

back towards the house, looking for signs of Diego and another assailant. They wouldn't have sent one man to grab him. That's when I heard it—a noise coming from the garage. It wasn't much, but it was enough for me to realize that's where the other guy was. I hugged the walls and ducked around corners as I made my way through the kitchen and into the garage. I paused just long enough to grab a small paring knife on my way. Most of you, and the people in movies, might grab a large knife. First of all, it doesn't take much to make a person bleed; second of all, a quiet, silent blade that no one sees is always better than a telegraphed large knife that someone can deflect.

The door from the kitchen to the garage was open and the light was on. I slipped to a room off to the side, just adjacent to the garage entrance. I was soaking wet, doing my best to be silent. I could hear the man searching for something specific. It didn't sound like he was looking for Diego, but some*thing* in particular. He was digging through boxes and other random stuff in the garage. I grew impatient after only a few minutes, so I leaned inside and saw him looking in a dark corner and opened the garage to startle him.

Now I had to think quickly. Do I double back, run around to the front, or wait for him in the house and see which way he runs? Lucky for me, the large man made it easy on me. He stood a little over six feet, wearing a dark hooded sweatshirt and matching sweatpants. He was a real winner. There are always things like this that even the other guys are embarrassed about. Let's be honest, anyone wearing sweatpants in general anywhere other than a bed or the gym is just weird. He took out a gun, aiming wildly, then when he accidentally knocked something over, he emptied a clip into the wall, shooting a tire. This gave me a chance to get into the garage without him noticing. I didn't quite run up on him, as he had me by a hundred and fifty pounds easy. I was still a little beaten up from the last guy and had to sneak up on this one.

I found myself ten feet from a man twice my size. Trying to avoid making any sloshing sounds, I slid out of my shoes, giving myself an edge. I crept up behind him with my small knife, stuck it in his side, then held it to his throat and pulled him to the ground.

"Where is Diego?!"

"Stupid bitch!" He winced.

"You're about to die. Go ahead and make that your last words. Or I can help you survive and call 911. Your choice." I probably won't, but hey.

"He's knocked out in the van. My partner is gonna kill you."

"Yeah, he's not going to. Sorry, but he's suffering a similar fate."

I laid him down while he held his side. It wasn't a cut deep enough to do major harm, just enough to hurt like a mother. He would survive, but he wasn't about to be running around anywhere. His partner was still out cold as I checked back through the house and doubled back to the van, which was now rocking.

Diego was inside rolling around, trying to free his hands, when I opened the door. The rain was beginning to pick up. I was somehow still getting wetter by the moment. "Hey babe, need a hand?" I whipped out the small knife and cut off the zip ties.

"Marie, how are you . . . Wait, there's another guy! There were two of them."

"He's out cold. I took care of him. Let's get out of here. We need to get out to where the girl is. I have a way to get her safe passage home without you catching any flack. But we need to go now."

Once I got Diego free from the zip ties, we shared a passionate kiss and a moment that finally calmed my anxiety. There's just something about the way he embraces me. It feels different. He has levels of passion, care, and motivation that drew me to him. I keep trying to hold myself back, knowing I'm in a vulnerable place, but I can't help it. I already have thoughts of trying to protect him as I bring down Andy and his shell game with the city's money.

"I need to do something real quick." Diego headed back into the house.

"Where are you going?" We needed to get out of here.

"I have to grab a few things and do something first."

He ran into his room, grabbed a bag, opened his safe, threw a few things in there and grabbed his gun. He tucked into his pants, something I had seen him do a few times. I didn't think anything of it. Then he asked me to grab the car and throw his bag in it. He wanted to check on the two guys, figure out who they were.

As I made it out to the car, I heard the first double-tap, then I heard another one. It was Diego finishing what I started. He did the thing I was afraid to do, the thing I couldn't do anymore. He quickly came outside, got into his Mercedes, and we pulled off. I was fully aware of what he had done, but I hadn't digested it yet. Who was going to clean it up? Was he just going to leave them there? Then again, he has a crew. I'm assuming he has people that can come clean up his house and make it like new all over again.

16

"Just keep your head down, keep calm, and trust me. This will be over soon, I promise."

We drove there in his car, a black Mercedes GLE coupe, brand new and gorgeous. The man has excellent taste—what can I say? It's not his fault he was thrown into this world; he's just doing his best to survive it. As soon as we hit the bridge, my heart started to beat a little bit faster. Though I knew we should have the upper hand, I couldn't help but be anxious. There was also an awkward silence in the car. I thought he would have more questions for me.

I couldn't help but focus on what happened back at the house. It had been long enough for me to work through the adrenaline of the attacks, the kiss that shook me, and the aftermath of him shooting the men that had probably still been out cold and defenseless. I wanted to bring it up, but I also wanted to focus on getting this girl. I knew that it wouldn't take much to get an answer out of him, since he knew I wasn't some dunce that he could get this over on.

It looks as though he's working through a few things too, that and a few phone calls to his top lieutenants to ensure they're still on his side and he hasn't lost anything. It also sounded like he was getting someone to head over to his place and clean up the mess he had just made. In fairness, Andy created this shit storm; Diego is just addressing everything as it's coming. I started texting Christian, letting him know what's going on. I told him to keep an eye out for us and know Diego is friendly.

"Okay, I think that's all the calls I needed to make." Diego looked at me. Here is my chance.

"Are we not going to talk about the double taps I heard before you got in the car? I know they weren't moving much, if at all." I crossed my arms.

"Andy isn't going to stop, and neither were they. There was no point in giving them a second chance, especially if you want to get away or make a run at anything else today. They would have called Andy and messed with our plans." Diego was focusing on the road, trying hard not to get a reaction from me.

"I guess I'll take that as a reasonable answer. Especially since you were tied up in the back of a truck. Is everything okay with the rest of your team? Or did Andy get to them already, assuming that he thought you'd be dead or in custody?"

"Nah, we're okay on my end; the people at the house are all my guys. None of them are with Andy. I tried to insulate them from the girl to ensure I could keep her safe. This whole thing is a mess; every time my life almost takes a shit, I find it has something to do with my old college buddy. Who were you texting?"

"The less you know, the better. It's just someone who is helping with the girl and with the money."

"Speaking of the money, Andy's guys kept saying you stole it. They knew we were working together, and that's why they came after me. Are you really involved with that?"

"We both hid a few things when we met. This was one of them. I didn't know you or Andy—"

Diego slammed on the brakes, skidding down the long highway bridge across Lake Pontchartrain. As the rain hit the windshield harder and harder, we began to hydroplane, swerving all over the road. Luckily for us, there weren't any other cars close to us. He was able to get the car back under control, pulled to the side, and put it in park. I thought he was going to lose it; I was prepared for it. Then he leaned in and kissed me again. I told you this guy is passionate.

"I was going to say I could kiss you, but I just did it instead. My hands moved quicker than my brain. I really don't care why, I'm just glad we have a way to pin this shit on him."

"I'll be honest, I didn't expect that. As for the money, the previous statement I said about knowing less still applies. You don't want to know about any of it. It's better this way. You're going to have to trust me."

"At this point, there is obviously a lot we don't know about each other. Let's get through this shit show and then we can go on a trip, get to know each other, and relax."

"Sounds like a plan to me; think we can get back on it? I have a small window to return the girl to her parents. Otherwise, we have a shot at being spotted."

Diego got us back on track, driving faster than ever. He was flying down the highway in the rain, with the car handling amazingly well. I guess it's true what they say about Mercedes: "The Best or Nothing." Arriving at the house, turning on the last road, I saw Diego tense up. I also received a message from Mike telling me that the local police were on their way; we needed to get in and get out

ASAP. We have maybe twenty minutes to get her and get going.

I shot Christian the same info to let him know what we were going to do and how quickly we needed to move. This girl needs to get home safe, priority number one. The second priority is keeping Diego's name out of all of this.

"Diego, I can't get into it, but we only have fifteen or twenty minutes to get the girl and get out. Authorities are going to be here soon; you need to get your guys out of there now."

"On it. I stopped worrying about why you know what you do. I'm just happy you're on my side right now." Let's hope I can protect him.

Diego was on the phone as we pulled up. One of his guys ran out the front door with the girl in hand and put her in the back seat. He threw a bag of her stuff in with her, and we pulled off. Diego was on the phone from the moment we pulled up until we got back on the bridge. He didn't even notice me hop in the back with her.

"We are taking you home to your family. You're safe now. But if you want this to go smoothly, you're going to have to keep how this rescue happened quiet."

I put my hand over her mouth to keep her quiet while Diego was on the phone, and to keep her calm. Once he was off the phone, I wanted to make her feel more comfortable.

"Hey, you can call me Sara. What's your name, sweetie?" I was using an old name I used to give guys I wasn't interested in.

"My name is Leslie. Am I going to be okay?" She was scared.

"Just keep your head down, keep calm, and trust me. This will be over soon, I promise."

As we were driving down the highway, Diego was focusing on the road as the rain had gotten even worse. I wanted to keep Leslie focused on something positive. I asked her how she was treated, mainly to see if Diego was truthful. She said the people who took her were mean, but the people at the house were very nice and kept reassuring her it would be over soon. They didn't want her to think her life was in danger; Diego was honest.

"Hey Diego, we need to head toward downtown. Give me your phone. I'll put an address close to where we are going in the GPS. Then we can drop her off a few houses away and she can walk up and be home."

"Smart idea; don't want to put her parents' address in my phone or yours. Sweetie, I promise we are going to get you home. This mess is almost over. Just hang in there."

Approaching the house, you could see her perk

up. She's not a little girl—I mean, she's almost a senior in high school. It's still a shit ordeal; we are taking a big risk allowing her to see our faces, but I'm trusting her father, and she just wants this to end. I'm covered either way, but I do worry about Diego; he has his hands dirty in plenty of places. I would be upset if he gets tagged with any of this, but it's the life he leads. I know it seems cold, but right now this girl is my top priority.

"We're almost there. Are you ready to get out, Leslie? We're going to drop you off two houses from yours. Then you can walk up."

"Yes, ma'am, thank you. I don't know who you are or how this is happening, but thank you."

"I'm just glad we could help."

She got out of the car, reached back in to grab her bag, and started running up the street. I texted Mike saying she'd been dropped off, then we went to the end of the street and parked. Diego and I got out of the car and watched. She knocked on her front door. You could see the excitement in her embrace with her mother.

That's when the crying started. Then Diego leaned into me, put his arm over my shoulders, and put his hand in mine. It was a positive moment in a day filled with shit. We got back into the car and just started driving. I needed a beer and a nap. I was drained mentally, but I knew it was just the start of the night. I kept feeling my phone go off but didn't think anything of it. I finally looked down to see multiple messages from Christian saying Andy and the local police showed up at the house.

"Diego, my contact just messaged me saying the cops are there now pulling that house apart. Is there anything in there to tie you to it?"

"No. We rented it from a local guy, paid him a ton of cash to keep it in his name. There's no receipt of the transaction. Come to think of it, I don't even think he's in the States right now. Is that all your contact gave you?"

"Nope. It looks like your good old buddy Schwartz was going to play the hero. But there was no one there for him to arrest," I said, laughing.

"Thanks to you and your contacts. Will I ever meet them?" Diego said with a frown.

"I don't know; they like their privacy, just like I do with my work being so sensitive and everything."

"I can understand that. Am I going to stay on your good side?"

"That's up to you; so far you're doing pretty good. How about we make it back to your place first and try to unwind a bit and then think about our next move?"

"Sounds good to me. We're almost there anyway."

We pulled in and rushed into the house, where we tore each other's clothes off. The downside of getting involved with someone on a case, especially in this high-stress environment, is that it can create a false sense of excitement in a relationship. I'm not quite sure where I am with Diego, but I can tell you we have fun together, and he makes me feel special.

Right now, with all that has been going on, it almost feels like winning the lottery. Even if I end up broke, giving this money back so it can be used properly, I'm not worried about where I'll end up. I am like a cat in that I always end up on my feet, always have. It's the tenacity I have, the preparation I put in, and the work ethic my dad instilled in me.

All tired out—more importantly, satisfied and relaxed—we laid on his bed, laughing. Still breathing heavily, it hurt a bit to be laughing at the same time, but we both had enormous smiles on our faces. Diego stood up to walk to the bathroom when I noticed again what a cute ass he has.

"Hey, thanks for that, babe."

"Not so bad yourself, Marie." Diego was grinning.

"I should probably get going, though. If I'm going to be able to pull this other thing off, I'm going to be working most of the night. The kind of people I need help from like to work when the rest of the world is sleeping."

"That's a good point, plus I need to get my guys together and confront Andy on this shit. No need in dragging it out, but I'm not going in there solo."

"Diego, be careful. He's a backstabbing asshole. At least text me when you're on your way and where. In case something happens, I'll know where to start looking."

"You're one different kind of gal. I like that about you."

As Diego was complimenting me and getting ready, I started the search around his place for my clothes. I was able to find my pants and shirt, but I was missing some underwear and a shoe. Not quite a full wardrobe, but I'm almost there.

"Hey, have you seen my other shoe, or my—"

"It's right here." He handed me my underwear in my shoe.

"Isn't that convenient? I'm going to head out." I put on my other shoe and stuffed my underwear in my back pocket.

"You're a little bit nuts and a whole lot awesome." Told you he's a sweetheart.

"Thanks, Diego. Let me know when it's all going down. Please be safe. I really like having you around."

"That makes two of us."

I walked out of his place, underwear and pride intact. I did it with my head held high. This badass crushed it tonight. We got that girl home safe and sound, and I got lucky. That's a double win for me; next up is getting the money to mess with Andy. Let's keep the ball rolling. Shit, my phone keeps going off. It's Neil. What does he need from me?

"Neil, did that girl get home safe? All good?" I know she got home.

"Yes, but there's still a slight problem!" What now?

17

"Does he know your real life yet?"

As soon as those words left Neil's mouth and traveled through the phone into my ears, my good night just stopped. Neil never beats around the bush; he's known for telling it like it is and just hammering it home. I can't wait to find out what the issue is.

"Neil, is the girl okay? That's my biggest concern right now."

"Yea, Marie, she's fine. The issue is with some shit Andy pulled."

"What did he go and do now? Is it related to the raid he pulled off on the other side of the lake?"

"That's the very same. He claims he has evidence and a witness that puts Diego and the girl in that house."

"She's home now, and they didn't find her there. Unless he has a picture of him and her together, isn't that accusation useless?"

"I'd normally say yes, but Andy still carries some weight under his more common name ... Councilman Schwartz."

"What about Wes? He knows Schwartz was behind this. Can't he help buffer some of the noise?"

"He's too afraid of what Schwartz might do. Right now, we still have him off the grid. We can pull him out, but are you ready to do that? Schwartz already kidnapped his daughter. You can't blame him for not wanting to risk anything else. "

"I mean, his daughter is home safe. Doesn't that mean we can?"

"It's only part of the equation. The other part is using the missing Rivers as someone to blame then corner Schwartz later, showing him that Rivers is alive and talking. I know the FBI would love to do that, especially if we find a way to get that money moved around."

"That's a good point. Neil, I guess we'll have to sell this money thing, won't we? I'll work on a plan tonight that we can try to put in play ASAP. Did TJ start moving the money around?"

"He did, and I have an idea for you as well so

that you're not drifting out there in the wind. Being a solo act is hard enough, but doing it without funds is brutal."

"What do you mean? I understand the sentiment, but what are you trying to tell me?"

"I think when this is all done, you should think about consulting with BCI. It'll give you access to funds and support that you need. We can help you build your own team down in New Orleans, something to grow with."

"I appreciate it, Neil. Let's get through this case and see how it ends. As for Andy, we need to have someone, maybe from the FBI, press the case and make him show the evidence. My guess is he has someone bought and paid for if he got that warrant to search the house without people questioning him."

"Our thoughts exactly. TJ's team is working with the FBI to find links between Schwartz and local judges. As a former district attorney and defense attorney, he's built a wide net of contacts in that world."

This went on for a few minutes, lots of conjecture and guessing until we finally hung up. We were on the call so long I was able to get in my car, drive across town, and even get changed. It was one of those conversations that you realize might take a while from the get-go. Now I was sitting in my place, with my tablet and phone out, connections under review. And I now had more pieces to add to the puzzle.

Andy's tree limbs kept growing as I mapped this out. He has connections all over, and most of them started in his youth. Most of these powerful men and women he is attached to start with their fathers. He has groomed these relationships over time. The question is, are the other people involved in this merely complicit, or are they active?

As I was trying to find a way to put pressure on Andy and his organization, I started worrying about Diego and Christian. I know they aren't together, but I haven't heard from either of them in a little bit. I decided to check in with Christian first, knowing he probably wouldn't answer. I'll get a text message if I'm lucky. He's one of those people that will ignore your call, then text you two seconds later. As expected, I called, it was ignored, and he messaged me saying he would call shortly.

Next, I turned my attention to Diego. I had yet to hear anything and was starting to get anxious, especially with the way Andy has been trying to put pressure on their relationship and show who's the boss. He's no Angela Bower, but he's definitely trying. I called him; no answer. That's not surprising, since he's busy working. That doesn't take the fear out of what's going on in my head, though. I decided to throw on some shoes and go for a run around the neighborhood. Even if it's late as shit and still a bit wet out.

I threw on my headphones and turned on *Glory Sound Prep* by Jon Bellion and started out the door. There is nothing quite like his tunes. I'm starting to sense a trend when I go running. Christian finally calls me back.

"Hey bud, how's your night going?" I was talking between breaths.

"Are you running, Marie? I can call you back."

"I am, but it's fine, let's multitask. How'd the night go? How was the scene with Andy at the house?"

"You could tell he was pissed. I mean, he was losing his shit all over the place. I even caught him kicking shit around, like a spoiled little rich kid. He really lived up to that moniker 'The Brat!'" Christian laughed at his own joke.

"If I weren't busy getting that girl home, I would've loved to have seen it. Anything else come out of it?" I was fishing.

"Actually, I think we know for certain who his contact is at the police chief's office. It's the deputy police chief. It sucks, too, 'cause she's had a hell of a career. The only thing I can think of is that he has some shit on her."

"I'll do some digging and see what I can come

up with. Any leads you came across when looking into the chief?"

"Actually, Marie, there is a place where you can start. She picks up her coffee at the Café du Monde out on Veterans Boulevard. Then out there in Harahan, where all the nice houses are, I can't remember exactly who, but she's related to someone high up. It's in my notes. I think TJ had it in an email he sent us. If you search her name, you'll find it."

"Thanks, Christian, I'll get on it when I get back to my place. I'm almost done."

"How's everything with you and Diego? Does he know your real life yet? He's a smart guy. He has to know something doesn't add up."

"I agree. I just don't think he cares right now. He wants Andy out of the picture as much as any of us. For now, the enemy of our enemy is our ally."

"Going all Sun Tzu on us, I see. At least I think that's where it's from."

"You're off hundreds of years; maybe more. It's Winston Churchill. My dad was a big military guy, and he loved his war history."

"Have a great night, Marie. Let me know how the morning goes."

"Will do. Have a great night, Christian."

Back at the house and dripping in sweat, I sat

down and started digging through emails from TJ on Vanessa Clark. There it is: the email he was talking about. It looks as if her family is somehow tied to the City Council and has been for years. They are business owners in the community, and are pretty successful, I might add. Big in real estate and a growing law firm. I wonder how she ended up in law enforcement.

She comes from a family that overcame a lot to earn their success. Being a Black family in the South is never easy—well, any minority for that matter. I highly doubt she would be going along with any of this shit unless Andy had some dirt on her. It just doesn't add up, the more I read on her and the community impact her family has made. I was getting lost in the case files, trying to see where she might have turned a corner, when Diego called.

"Marie, I've only got a minute, but I'm going to text you an address. I'm on my way there, but I'm a bit concerned. It turns out Gaines is in town. He wants to meet up without Andy."

"That might be a good thing. He wants to work with you on the project and get past dealing with an incompetent asshole." Diego laughed a bit, but it was an uneasy laugh.

"Funny as that is, Gaines is a psychopath. He just got out of prison a little bit ago, and he's already raising hell over everything. He wants this rollout to go perfectly. New Orleans is important to him for some reason. It's almost as key as Detroit is. I just don't know why."

"Want me to be in the area in case something happens? I don't have to be there, but I can be close."

"If you don't hear from me in an hour, even a text, then call LT immediately and give him the address. He's worried too, but I'm not supposed to bring anyone to the meeting."

"You got it. Be safe, Diego. I'll talk to you in a bit."

"'Bye, babe."

I got off the phone and changed immediately. I didn't even take the time to shower. I did throw on some deodorant, though. I'm not a savage. I might not be fresh, but I'm not going in au naturale. If I'm going to try and be covert, I can't have people smelling me from across the room. As I ran out of the room, I grabbed a small tracker and then took a minute to call Christian and have him meet me over there. The address is out on the West Bank, some town called Algiers. It's one of the oldest neighborhoods in the area, according to my phone.

This is one of the reasons I'm down here in the first place. We had a feeling Gaines would make a bigger play on New Orleans and the group he was using to move product. Taking money and causing havoc was all about poking the hornet's nest to see if he would poke his head out. It looks like tonight is that time. I had to get close and keep an eye on Diego. There is no telling what Gaines would do. He's never afraid to cut a loose tie.

As I got close to the address, I realized this wasn't a warehouse or anything like that; it's new construction. There is already a restaurant and some dental place in a strip. The address seems to be one of the spaces in the middle that are under construction. I shot Christian a text to see where he was. I got back, "Perched across the street." I'm not even going to ask how he beat me here. I'm just going to be glad I have cover for a change.

I pulled the car to the edge of the parking lot, with my lights off. There were already a couple of cars from the looks of it, probably the workers closing the restaurant next door. I should be good to keep an eye on everyone. Even though they're working in the dark, you can see them clearly enough. I took out my phone and attached a camera extension; though not perfect, it does give me some range. Watching the meeting go down, I could feel my heart beating, getting ready for what was to come.

Five minutes in, I could see that the body language was changing between the two men. I only wish I could hear them, know what's being said. From the looks of it, Diego is going to be in trouble. Two guys are standing behind him. With Gaines getting more and more heated, I could see Diego's body language become more defensive and tense. I decided to call Christian.

"Hey Christian, are you seeing this?"

"Yeah, Gaines looks angry as shit in there. Did Diego bring any backup?"

"You're looking at it. He doesn't know I'm this close, but he told me where he was going to be."

"You two are really building up trust, aren't you?"

"That's what I'm good at. It's my job." And I think I'm falling for him.

"Well, you might want to think fast. Gaines just slugged him, and his two buddies grabbed him."

"I'm watching with my camera attachment. I wish I could hear them. If Gaines is just trying to send a message, I don't want to risk breaking cover. If he's going to kill him, that's a whole 'nother issue."

"I don't see anyone grabbing guns right now. I think you'll be okay. But we need to be ready to extract him. He's our best contact for mitigating what Gaines is trying to do in New Orleans with Andy."

"No shit, Christian! Sorry—just hard to watch someone get their ass kicked like this."

After fifteen minutes of watching Gaines wail on my Diego, I couldn't take it anymore. I was beginning to get myself ready for a frontal assault that might get both of us killed. Lucky for me, Gaines backed off finally, maybe out of exhaustion, and let Diego catch his breath. He was beaten up pretty badly from what I could see. I took one more breath and waited to see Gaines's next move. He looked as if he was done.

He walked out the back door with his security detail and left Diego there to suffer. As soon as I saw Gaines had left, I drove around the back to try and get in the back door. It was locked. Diego was inside, unable to move, and I couldn't get in. I went to the back of my car, found the tire iron, and pried open the door. It wasn't pretty, but it was effective.

"Diego, are you okay? Diego?"

I ran inside and found him unconscious, bleeding all over. I should have come in sooner. I should have tried to save him. I know I can't take him to the ER. I needed to call LT and find out what to do. I sat there, fighting back tears, trying to get my thoughts together as I dialed LT.

"LT, I . . . I . . . "

"Marie, what's going on? Is Diego okay?"

"No, he's not. He's in bad shape. Where should I take him? I'm assuming he doesn't want to go to the ER."

"There's a clinic we go to, a doctor near his place. I'll text you the address and meet you over there. Do you need help getting him in the car?"

"No, I can do it."

18

"This isn't going to take a few hours."

By the time I got off the phone with LT, Christian was already behind me. He began helping me carry Diego into the car. Diego was out cold. He was breathing, but it was extremely shallow. He probably had a broken rib or two. Every time he forced in a larger breath, he would wince, though I still couldn't get his attention. I couldn't get him to acknowledge anything that was going on.

Christian followed me from a safe distance since I still had my tracker active. I was filled with anxiety the whole drive over there, as one might expect with a bleeding man in your front seat. It took nearly thirty minutes to get across the bridge and over to the address LT had sent. Diego was lucky in that the majority of his cuts weren't deep. They were simply from getting beaten up, not stabbed or shot.

This kept the mess to a minimum, but it was still bad. It's not like I could lie my way out of this if I was pulled over. The building at the address from LT looked like a warehouse, not like anything related to a doctor. Something seemed fishy. I called Christian to have him go around the building and see what he could see while I sat in the car.

"Hey Christian, what are you seeing?"

"It's not looking good. My guess would be LT is changing teams to Andy instead of Diego. This looks like an old-fashioned ambush. Get out of there now!"

"What?! I'm confused. Why would LT do this? Are you sure?"

I could see LT getting closer, walking ever so gently to the car. He had a big smile on his face, but all I could hear was Christian telling me to get out of there. I began quickly going over my options. I texted Uncle Phil and told him I needed a doctor ASAP, someone off-book. He messaged back an address almost instantly. LT was moving close enough to open the car door, from the looks of it.

I put the address in my phone and peeled out, running over LT's foot in the process. I could hear him screaming and yelling a few choice words behind me. I needed to make sure I lost LT and his crew quickly and get Diego to this address ASAP. He was starting to come to, but he was still mumbling mostly. Once he heard LT screaming, he came to like a bolt of lightning; most likely, adrenaline grabbed him by the collar.

"Marie, what was that? Did you just drive over LT?"

"Diego, I'm taking you to a doctor I know; the place LT brought me to isn't what it seems. He said this was your doctor when shit like this happens. I'm positive he's working with Andy too."

"What the hell is going on? No, this isn't even the right part of town, my doctor is on the west bank." I knew it.

"Well, I'm heading to an off-book doctor as we speak to get you fixed up. Are you going to be okay?"

"I've had my ass kicked worse than this plenty of times. I'll be okay."

"Diego, can you tell me why that guy was beating you up, and who he is?" I know it's Gaines, but I'm still playing a part.

"His name is Jason Gaines. He's the head of all this shit. Andy reports directly to him and me to Andy. It looks like I'm the fall guy for all Andy's mishaps. After I told Gaines the truth about what

Andy did, kidnapping that girl, Gaines was pissed."

"If he's a drug dealer, a cold-blooded type, why would he care?"

"Gaines is a lot of things, but to him, kids and families are always off-limits. For a crazy person, he has some code of ethics, I guess. I'm not sure he always follows it, but he'll enforce it. As for this doctor, can they be trusted?"

"They can, but I need to make a call."

I called Christian via Bluetooth and kept any eye on my rearview mirror. As the city faded in the background and the highway into the wetlands, I kept checking in. Christian said my tail was clear. It looks like they didn't even bother to follow us once we left the city. We both assumed they weren't planning on hopping back in their cars, just expecting us to walk in and be served up on a platter.

Neither Christian nor I were aware of where we were going. It was the middle of nowhere, according to the GPS. Uncle Phil had messaged us saying it's a safe house he had set up when this job came up in case of a situation like this. The doctor we are going to see will meet us in a van a few miles off the main road and bridge.

We are headed into swamplands on the basin, which covers a huge portion of land out here. Well, it's mainly water, houses that have seen better days, and a shit ton of airboats. A lot of things were racing through my mind. I only wish I had time to write them down and organize them into something that made sense. I'm quick at making decisions and staying calm, but not always great about keeping the details together.

My first question is, when did doctors become mobile? In vans, no less. I messaged Uncle Phil for more details about the van. He was still waiting. He said they change the look of the vehicle to keep it from being too obvious. I guess that makes sense, but it's still odd. As my thoughts were drifting in and out of so many details, I received a message saying it's a mobile dog washing van. Oh, great.

The second issue I have is with this whole scenario. I'm going to have to tell Diego the truth, or at least some semblance of it. Christian is going to be a huge part of allowing me to keep an eye on Diego as he recovers. Even if he's a badass movie type, he's going to need a few days to recoup. This isn't going to take a few hours. like just getting a nap in and throwing some tape on. That shit isn't real; hell, I once sprained an ankle on a case and had to be sidelined for a week.

The other issue that was picking at me tirelessly was how I am going to take down Gaines and Andy. I really hope TJ has some answers for us with the money. If we can remove at least one piece from the chessboard, maybe we can maneuver a little better. I knew this case was going to be a pain in the ass. Then again, those are the best ones for me, especially now. Having the shitty opinion of myself that I do allows me to make decisions I normally wouldn't.

The only issue I'm going to run into is if I have to kill someone. I can't right now. Everything with Maria is still fresh in my mind. It's more than the act itself, or the fact that she was one of the few people that has trusted me, known my secrets. It was the closeness, the personal nature of how it went down. When you are that close to someone as you do that, especially when they are no threat to you, it's hard to cope. There are no mental gymnastics to rationalize that behavior, unlike when your life is being threatened. That is your out: You had to defend yourself. The situation with Agent Garcia and Susie Gaines didn't have that. It's why I'm still struggling.

"Hey Marie, who are you texting and calling so much?"

"Diego, there will be plenty of time for storytelling. Right now, I'm trying to get you some help and get you to a safe place. I'm one of the few people on your side right now, and you need to trust me."

Just like that, he started fading in and out again, struggling to talk. He could barely keep his eyes open as he was wincing with each breath. As we pulled off the last bridge, I saw a van on the side of the road with a big dog decal on the side. I hope this is our doc. I don't think Diego is going to make it much farther.

Christian pulled up and walked to the van to make sure it was safe. As he waved me down, I felt a wave of relief. We were in the middle of nowhere, with no cars or lights for miles. It was just us, a shit ton of bugs, and plenty of swamp creatures. The noises from the darkness would scare even the sanest of people. Christian helped me carry Diego over to the van. As the doors opened, it looked like an ambulance on the inside.

"Hey doc, nice setup here. How'd you get involved in this kind of shit?" I'm nervous, old small talk habits kicking in.

"Well, miss, I did plenty of tours overseas as a medic, came back to be a doctor, and missed the excitement. That's how I ended up doing this. I still have a practice, but I help out old Lady Liberty and her coworkers from time to time." That's a poetic way of saying it.

"He needs our help; a big case is dependent on him staying alive." And I'm falling for him.

"Well, give me about thirty minutes here, and

I'll see what I can do. But there's only enough room in here for the patient and me. Can you please close the door? You also might want to pull your cars off into the brush somewhere, so it's not so obvious."

"Got it!"

Christian pulled up the street about a block to keep an eye on traffic, and I went the other way. I wasn't nearly as far, but I was also staring directly at the van, waiting for it to open. While I was waiting for the doctor to finish up with Diego, I pulled my tablet out of my backpack. I started going through the case, the connections and moving LT, and a few others over to the Andy and Gaines side. I was trying to see how many, if any, Diego still had on his.

He treats his crew excellently and doesn't nickel-and-dime them, so I can assume he has a strong following. The problem is that in this game, money speaks loudly, sometimes louder than loyalty. Just short of an hour later, I had a revised tree, and plenty of questions to go over with Diego about it that would help me blow this case wide open. We need to find the pressure points to topple Gaines and his organization.

I saw the back door open, and as I ran over to help Diego out, I could see he was smiling. He looked at me passionately and with the same level of trust Maria once did. I started to flash back emotionally to that moment, causing my eyes to well up with tears.

"Hey Marie, I'm going to be fine. The doctor says I have some fractures—well, plenty of them—and I need to rest. I'll be okay. We can talk about everything else later. For now, we need to find a place to lay low."

"I'm sorry, it's just been a rough day. I have a place for us, in the middle of nowhere; we can talk more there. Let's get in the car and get you some rest." I was still fighting back the tears.

"Miss, here are some pain pills for him, as well as some anti-inflammatory meds. He needs to lay low for a few weeks. I'm assuming it'll barely be a few days, but rest is the key for him." The doc gets it.

"Got it. Thank you for everything."

"That's what I'm here for. Good luck with your case." He handed me a black card with an email address and walked away.

With Diego in the car, beginning to get some rest from the painkillers, I backed out and waited for Christian to turn around. With the two of us driving in tandem, we followed the GPS farther and farther into the thick of the wilderness. The swamp grew bigger and the road smaller as we navigated through the night. By now it was nearly three in the morning; I know I was exhausted, as

Christian must be too.

Finally, we made it to the house, if you can call it that. Christian helped me get Diego inside; he was barely functioning. The house had only three rooms, a bathroom, and a kitchen area. It was simply a sink and a bag of charcoal for a small grill by the back door. There was a bedroom with one bed in it, and a few cots set up in the corner.

Living the spy life, you get used to shit living situations. I've slept on the floor or in closets on more than one occasion. Closet, you ask—well, I'm small and fit into tight spots. Sometimes a closet hidden under some clothes is a safe place, and not just for a cat. While Christian began unloading gear, I did my best to talk to Diego so he didn't wake up confused or scared.

"Diego, we need to talk. I just need you awake for a minute or two."

"I'm here, I swear. My eyes are closed but I'll repeat, so you know I understand."

"There is a guy here, a friend of mine who helped me save you. His name is Christian, and he's just a friend. We can trust him. When you wake, don't worry, we'll be here for you. If you need anything, I'll be in the other room."

"Okay ... Christian ... he's good ... got it." Diego softly repeated me as he fell asleep.

I walked out of the room, closing the door ever

so gently. He was going to need lots of rest. Recovering from that kind of beating is about time and sleep. I'll keep checking on him, but for now I'm going to touch base with Christian and check my phone. Son of a bitch, we have no service out here—not surprising.

"Christian, I'm assuming you're like me, with no signal?"

"Yeah, no shock there. I lost the signal about ten minutes out. I was digging around the cabinets and checking for any signs of Wi-Fi. There's a satellite in a tree out back with cables running into the house. There has to be some form of signal around here."

"Sounds right, plus Uncle Phil is the kind of guy that would set it up first. Maybe if we follow the cable back to the house, we can see where it's hooked up and start from there. I'll go look, and you keep unpacking." I grabbed a flashlight out of my car and started walking around the house. With each step there was a bit of a squish, like I'm walking on a sandbar in Florida.

With little light and lots of bugs attacking me as if I were invading their country, I finally found the box. I popped it open with a knife. Inside I found a note from Uncle Phil.

Hey Marie, if you're reading this, it's not a good day. Wi-Fi password is your birthday and father's initials, all caps.

Isn't he a crafty one? Now that I have that in tow, I turned it on at the box and went back inside. I found Christian asleep on one of the cots in the corner—also not surprising, as it's been a long night. I wrote down the Wi-Fi info for him, grabbed my tablet, and logged onto the Internet. It was time to go over my notes one more time before falling asleep. And now to figure out how to have *that* tough conversation with Diego, the one I've dreaded for so long.

19

"I just feel like your vision might be skewed on this."

W here do we go from here? I barely slept, but was able to charge my phone and tablet. At least I have that going for me, since I fell asleep with them on my chest. Christian seemed to sleep as much as I did; he was in the kitchen trying to find coffee and anything else. He decided to run into town and track down some items while I stayed here and kept an eye on Diego.

With Christian gone, I decided to get Diego up and try to get him a shower. The bathroom was the size of a closet. It had just enough room for a stand-up shower and the usual suspects. It had a small toilet, oddly low to the ground, and a tiny pedestal sink. There wasn't even a mirror, just a small shelf for bringing your own, I can only assume. As I rolled him over and up, I put his arm over my shoulder and moved him to the shower, slowly getting him undressed as we walked.

Once the water hit him, he began to come to. He was mumbling and muttering some things and occasionally slamming his fist into the tile wall. I was trying to help him but could tell he was just getting frustrated, since he was wincing in pain with each punch.

"Diego, what do you need from me?"

"I just need a few minutes to work through this shit and clear my head and find a way to get to Andy sooner rather than later."

"I'll just be outside if you need anything. We'll figure this out together."

"Wait, you don't need to go. Who is this guy who helped you—I mean, helped us?"

"His name is Christian. He works with a company out of Detroit. I was up there working a few months ago; that's where we met. He's down here helping me. He's part of a group I'm working with to take down Gaines." Shit, that came out quicker than expected.

"Wait—take down Gaines? Are you law enforcement or some shit? I knew something was up. You're too talented to be a street kid. LT told me he didn't like you. It's probably why he sided with Andy in all this shit." I couldn't tell if he was in pain, or pissed.

"You had a feeling early, and it didn't bother you? Or you didn't show it, at least." That's why we probably connected. Like I said, we both knew we were liars.

"Marie, come on. You're one in a million. I knew you were some agent or ex-military when you helped me at the house. You took down that big-ass guy, then freed me. It's not difficult to realize you're more than meets the eye. I was holding out hope you were some burned spy or someone who had nowhere to go. You're not investigating me, are you?" His look is a mix of concern and a little bit of anger.

"Came here to infiltrate the group working with Gaines, mainly Andy. You and LT were just a way to get to them. You were never part of what I was looking into. No, I'm not anything really. I'm not a spy, I'm just a hired gun to do shit no one wants to take blame for. I'm expendable. Are you pissed? Where does this leave us?" Asking for a friend.

"I can't think straight about us. I need to get Andy and figure this shit out. He keeps jacking up my life. I'm sick and tired of it. Are we good? No! Are we bad? No! I don't know what to think. I still love the shit out of you. But I can only be lied to so much by so many people in my life." Did he just say love?

"I get it. I never meant to hurt you or anyone around you. Andy perhaps, and now LT. Let's focus on getting your life straight; at the end, if you want me gone, I'll leave. If you want me around, I'll stay."

"Right now, I want Andy gone as badly as you do. Gaines, to me, is just a business deal. At this point it sounds like he's siding with Andy, according to the beating I took." He was pissed, and at this point, I wasn't sure who he was most upset with.

"Is that what all the shit was about?"

"I don't know how to explain this easily. But I'll try, Marie."

After he got out of the shower and wrapped himself in a towel, he just sat in the bathroom, and I stood in the doorway as we talked. He explained to me how he came to know Gaines, how the two of them have had an understanding. His deal is with Andy, but it was Diego's job to keep Andy in line. It wasn't as if he and Gaines had a long relationship. It was a few conversations and an agreement. He would do business in New Orleans and with Andy only if Diego could keep it under control.

It seems obvious that people continually put up with Schwartz because of his connections and his money. If we get a hold of those, remove those variables, he'll be ours for the taking. Diego agreed that Gaines is a longer play, harder to take down. But if we can remove Andy and his network from the field, then we have a better shot. We had talked for almost an hour when Christian finally came back.

"Hey there, Diego, I'm Christian. Nice to finally talk to you. I bought some clothes for you. I hope they fit. I figured all the torn and damaged ones might need to be replaced." Diego was still in a towel.

"Thanks, bud. I appreciate it."

Christian tossed him a pair of jeans and a Nickelback T-shirt. Diego is more a fan of linen or a nice pair of dress pants, but I don't think they have a vast selection out here. I'm not sure where he found the T-shirt, but I'm not going to lie, it's funny and cute on Diego at the same time. I mean Nickelback hasn't been relevant for years, and they are one of those bands we all love to hate. They sing that catchy pop shit that gets stuck in your head.

"Christian, where did you find that T-shirt? The best part is it's a little tight on him." Which I'm enjoying.

"It was at a gas station on my way out of here to find food and some supplies. All that was in the fridge were some bottled waters, meal replacement bars, and energy gummies. They were great for a pre-workout, but we might need some food if we're going to be out here laying low for a few days."

"I'll take anything I can get. Thanks, Christian. Marie, do you think I can have water and one of those bars before I lay back down? My ribs are killing me, but I need something in my stomach." Diego slowly changed and walked over to the bedroom.

"I got you; lay down. I'll bring over your pain meds and something to eat. Do you need to charge your phone?"

"No, I have one of those juice pack cases, so I'm still good. I'll need to eventually, just not now."

Diego laid down while Christian and I walked the five steps to the kitchen area. Okay, maybe it was more like ten, but this place is small. My dorm room felt bigger than this. Then again, I had a different perspective than I do now.

I took care of Diego with water and a meal replacement bar. He laid down, got on his phone, and started reaching out to guys. I really needed to talk to him about the network Gaines and Andy have, plus their connections. If he knows I'm in this for some reason other than his affection, I should be able to get information out of him. He is balanced. It's always about give and take. If it's a great deal, he's okay with it as long as he doesn't feel like he is getting screwed. That is, unless it's by a sexy woman, such as myself.

Christian and I talked softly, started calling our contacts, and worked the network we have. TJ and his team at BCI were working on the connections between Gaines and Andy, while I worked up the courage to talk to Diego again. He had fallen asleep after messaging a few of his crew and calling two others while Christian and I worked in our small space, doing our best not to trip over each other.

Luckily for us, there was one small window AC unit keeping the space bearable, though it needed help from an old metal fan on the floor. Its hum was a loud reminder of the situation that we were operating in.

"Christian, do you think TJ is ever going to get that money moved around? That's going to be the big play to push this. Also, did Neil give you any advice? He's always great at seeing things differently."

"The first answer is that TJ said the money transfers take time. He needs a few more days; otherwise it's going to look obvious. He needs to get a paper trail put together, access some bank statements, and make the proper notes. It's essentially forgery, but for a good purpose. Neil said he should have some more info for us by tomorrow." Christian looked a bit ticked.

"Are you all right Christian? You look mad."

"I know you like Diego, and you think he can be an asset, but I just feel like your vision might be skewed on this. I trust you—I have to. Other than one case, you have a great track record."

"What do you mean? Did you do some digging on me? There's a good chance this is the end of our partnership anyways. Consider my vision clear."

"It was part of the deal. I got to read your dossier and get a feel for who I was working with. You've done some ballsy shit, done a lot of good. It's why I volunteered to come out here. The Santa Fe thing is a blip on the radar compared to everything else you've done."

"That means a lot, Christian, but I can tell you right now it's more than a blip."

"I know you've taken it pretty hard. Our jobs aren't easy. We make the calls we think are right. It doesn't mean they will all work out. That's part of the burden of people like us, and you must carry more than most." Christian has a point.

"I'll do my best to prove to you and the whole BCI team, especially Neil, that I can make up for that. I may never be able to erase the pain, but I can make sure it wasn't for nothing."

"We know, Marie. Each day will be a new opportunity to move forward. It'll take time."

PERDUE

Christian and I went back and forth, talking about the case, talking about Santa Fe, and eventually I got tired of it all. I realized the only way I was going to get anywhere was to talk to Diego. I was tired and mentally drained from watching someone I care about beaten to a pulp and left for dead. Had I not called LT, I think they would have thought he was dead in Algiers right now.

They wouldn't think he was holed up with his girlfriend somewhere laying low. They wouldn't be trying to figure out their next move with him out there. They would be more concerned with their drug trade and the purchase from Gaines. I keep second-guessing every move, every decision; I can't function like this. I never used to be this way. I would go with my decision and trust it, regardless of the world around me.

I decided to go into the room and lay down with Diego. He was sleeping, but just being in there will calm me down. Laying down next to him and breathing in unison with him, the rhythm has a calming effect on me. By now you know that I like him more than just a guy I'm dating. He treats me special, doesn't judge me, and enjoys me for who I am, not for who I can be. You might not understand how hard that is for a girl, but most of our lives are about being someone we are supposed to be. It's rarely about being the woman we want to be. We are always changing or adapting for the people in our lives, making concessions in our personalities.

After a few hours of lying next to him, lost in thought, I kept rolling over and curling up with him. Then I would hear him wince and pull back, causing me to stop. It's hard because when we normally sleep together, I wrap myself up in his arm, tucked into his shoulder. That makes me feel safe, puts me in a zone of sorts. I need that right now, but he can't give that to me since he's so fragile. Eventually he woke up and started asking me questions. He could tell I was struggling with something.

"Marie, I can tell when you're hiding something by now." Diego wasn't holding back.

"Diego, it's something that happened a while back. On my last case when I was in New Mexico. I did something . . . something so unforgivable, I can't bring myself to even bear it. It weighs on me so much it has me questioning every move I make." The tears started almost instantly.

"Marie, you are one of the most amazing women I have ever met. Regardless of where we stand or end, I still care about you. If you are carrying such baggage, the only way to overcome it is letting someone help you with the burden. I have plenty of skeletons in my closet; let me in. I'll carry it with you. You saved my life, gave me a second chance." Shit, this really is the end of my secrets with Diego.

"You still haven't asked me what I do or who I work for. Do you want to know?"

"As long as you're not DEA or local police, I don't care. You can tell me when you're ready." He laughed and caught his side from pain.

"I don't work for either of them. I have never been a police officer and consulted on a case with the DEA only once. I don't know why I told you that, but it's true."

"What's weighing on your heart, bringing you down?"

We talked for the next—who knows? I really don't anymore. I was lost in the emotion of explaining to him everything that happened in Santa Fe. The way I took someone's love from them, how they handled it, and the pain I feel daily. He kept reassuring me that life has a way of throwing us baggage, especially for those of us who work in the shadows. He was starting to sound like Christian.

It doesn't make it okay, but it does put it into perspective. It's like my dad used to say; if you dealt drugs in your youth, but grew up in the projects, it's not a crime. He would call that a first job, and he was dead serious. On the flip side, he would say if you got caught selling your parents' meds, you're an idiot. He understood that context and the variables in our situations matter. Our decisions don't operate in a bubble. Just as I was about to fall asleep, settle into Diego, and relax, Christian came running in.

"Guys, I hate to break this . . . whatever this is, up. But we need to talk right now."

"What's going on?" I damn near shot up.

"TJ and Neil were able to work with the FBI and round up charges on Andy. They have him on racketeering and kidnapping. Neil did an interview with the girl, found out where they kidnapped her from, and had TJ dig up footage around the area. They were able to get Andy's dumb ass at the scene of the crime."

"That's great news, but we still have some loose ends to tie up. What about LT, Jason Gaines, and the Requiem heading to New Orleans?"

"That's what Neil needs from us. He needs us to find out what leverage LT has and how it all plays into Gaines and the purchase. The biggest thing we need is to figure out when and where this purchase is going down."

"I can tell you guys that. Knowing Gaines, he hasn't changed shit. He's an arrogant asshole that is dumb enough to keep the same schedule." Diego slowly sat up.

"When and where?" I was frantic.

"What day is it? Wait, never mind, I remember now. It's going down tonight at midnight on the docks. He's using his connections and international shipping from Argentina to bring it into the States. That's why New Orleans is so important."

"Then let's get going. We need to get out there and scout it. Do you know where, exactly? The port is massive—that's like saying 'somewhere on the beach.'" Christian was getting excited.

"Yes, I have it saved in my phone. I wonder what LT might do if I tell him he's walking into a trap, but I can give him a way out."

"That's not the worst idea. Maybe we can have you play that role. We can convince him that you died. Then we can startle Gaines and his goons with an unveiling. It will help misdirect and keep them off balance."

"Let's put it together, Marie, but we have only a few hours to make a plan." Diego was concerned.

"This is how we operate. Christian and I will take care of everything, plus we have a secret weapon in town."

"What's that?" Diego looked confused.

"It's not a what. It's a who." Christian and I laughed and said it in unison: "Neil!"

20

"My lies are always too big to get over."

Diego was in the seat next to me, texting while I was driving. I was about to call LT and get the ball rolling on our plan. This was going to be fun. These are the moments I live for, the ones that get me out of bed in the morning. It's that scene in the movie when one guy walks into a room and tosses a gun to his buddy and says something catchy. Let's hope he picks up.

"I'm surprised you're calling me. Especially after that shit you pulled last night."

"Calm down, LT. I was trying to save Diego's life, and I was pretty sure you were setting me up."

"Did you succeed? The word on the street is that he's trying to find out who's still on his side."

"That's me using his phone. He died from

Gaines's beating and the shit his boys did." I started crying a bit, but these tears were all fake.

"Serves him right. He didn't see it coming. He thinks he's the brains." I had to keep Diego quiet.

"Well, we both know this is the Gaines and Andy Show, always has been, always will be. Gaines needs Andy's connections all over to make this work."

"Not sure what you think this whole thing has been about, but sure, you can believe that. It's not my job to catch you up to speed. Not to mention, what the hell does Diego's piece of ass care about his business now that he's gone?"

"I'd like to know what got him killed. It's not like we knew each other for a long time, but I cared about him. You wouldn't understand—it's a girl thing. We can get attached quickly. I guess if you don't know, then that's fine." Click. I hung up.

I knew he'd call back. I was hoping he would call Diego's phone so I could answer it. That way, I could make him think I was the one sending those messages this whole time. It didn't take but thirty seconds for Diego's phone to start ringing with LT's name scrolled across the caller ID.

"Hey LT, I knew you'd call me here, trying

to see if I was telling the truth. What's next?"

"I'll call you later. If you really want to know what all this is about, maybe we can work out a trade."

"Okay, but—" He hung up on me this time.

That's my move, and he turned it around on me. Then again, I'm not too concerned, since I'm the one holding cards they don't know I have. Diego was visibly pissed, even more than earlier. We started spitballing ideas for the port, how to work it to cover as many angles as we could at once, and whether I should call some more contacts to get them involved. While we talked, he kept finding ways to drop lines about how he can't trust anyone. He mentioned he's a lone man out there, with nobody but himself in his corner. I've seen this before, gone through it enough times to know. It doesn't matter that we thought we had something real. My lies are always too big to get over.

This is less about needing help and more about courtesy and respect for their investigation into Gaines Chemical with the FBI and the DEA. If I were out on my own, I know how I would place this. I would work with Diego and his team to get in there and flush out the drugs to a place another agency would have better access to. I'm more of an orchestrator that aids others in obtaining the knowledge and evidence needed to prosecute. Then I disappear into the dark places where the worst reside.

For now, I need to get Diego back to his place, where he is meeting the guys who are still loyal to him. He has a lieutenant named Pan, who is as vicious as she is beautiful. At least, I think she's a lieutenant of his. Diego said something once about her being placed in his ranks. When I asked him about it, he brushed it off.

She attended St. John's in New York, only to leave after her sophomore year. She ended up in New Orleans on a trip and never left, eventually meeting Diego and his crew and working her way up the ranks. He's probably better off with her as a lead than he ever was with LT. She is loyal to a fault and is much smarter than LT. He was more of a yes man. I still don't know if Pan is a nickname or her real name; no one will tell me. I asked a few different times and was ignored, so I just dropped it.

She's not that slender, petite type like me. She has some fitness to her, some curves. She is the daughter of parents who immigrated to the States some thirty years ago and met in New York, half Chinese and half Dominican. Needless to say, she grew up rough. The other thing I know is she doesn't like me. Right now, I'm grasping at straws, and Diego said to trust her to rally the troops. I reached out to her through his phone, telling her it was me. We never got along, not well, at least. I told her to get anyone to the house that's loyal to Diego; we had to go avenge Diego's death. I didn't want it getting out just yet. If we have them all in one place we can try and control the message.

Still, I don't like the idea of putting our faith in Pan. The story the crew gave me mixed with what Diego told me about how she ended up in the operation don't add up. I know it was a one-off, one time. I didn't think twice about it before. After Gaines kicking his ass, LT trying to kill him, and a chunk of his crew jumping ship, I'm worried. Then again, I'm the paranoid outsider; they trust her. I only have to trust Diego, not her.

With Diego back at his house and with his crew, it was time for me to head back to my place, clean up, and get ready for tonight. I was going to circle back with Diego in an hour or so. We both needed time to get organized and work out this evening's festivities with Gaines. On my way back to my place, I reached out to Neil, looking for some advice and asking how he wanted to play it.

"Neil, it's Marie. Has Christian touched base with you yet?"

"Yeah, he gave me the heads up. I looped in Mike from the FBI to see what they can do, if anything. Simply a tip isn't always enough to get a warrant, especially when dealing with an international port like New Orleans. This shit isn't a TV show where you can call a buddy and get a warrant in minutes."

"I know. It cracks me up how people can think the system moves that quick. It takes people like us working in the gray to move things along. Well, you work in the gray, I'm a bit more in the shadows."

"I can agree with that. Give me, like, thirty minutes to get an answer from Mike, and I'll call you. But I do think you need to have a presence there and find a way to stop this big deal."

"My theory is that Gaines has confidence in his ability to distribute. If we can impact that confidence in the community he's dealing to, it will help slow him down. His organization is so big that it's not as simple as taking him down. It's about cutting off limbs of the tree, then working our way to the roots, to his foundation."

"Well said, Marie. We're essentially on the same page. I'll call you shortly. If you don't hear from me, just use your best judgment. It means the FBI and other agencies are dragging their feet, which you're familiar with."

"Thanks, Neil."

I got into the shower quickly, cleaned up, and even had time to relax and let the water rush over me. I know what you're thinking, but I need to have my mind right, feel confident for what is ahead. Especially now, with my pixie haircut, the after-shower routine has sped up dramatically. Though I truly loved having my long hair, this allows me efficiency and options.

The choice I need to make when I get dressed is whether I should toss on a wig or keep my hair as-is. I know I bought the wigs to help, but I've been digging this hair. I haven't broken them out much, if at all. If I were lucky enough to have my story made into a movie or Netflix show, they'd probably have me dressing up in heels and a dress, or some miniskirt shit. Who are you kidding? If you ever have to run in heels, or duck from bullets, no thank you. I can look sexy and comfortable at the same time.

All dressed and ready to go, I started loading up my backpack with a few guns and extra ammo. I even went out to my Jeep to check on my rifle and rounds; this could get ugly quickly. It's not like I can walk in there like Schwarzenegger or Stallone in the movies. It might be a bit obvious if I have an M-16 on my back along with a belt of ammo.

I was feeling anxious and excited at the same time heading toward Diego's place. Moments like these are where I thrive, the stress and decisions that will be laid out in front of me. That's where I do my best work. The long investigations are tough for me. That's why I take so many notes and work through them, stay organized, and plan.

By the time I had arrived at Diego's, the parking lot and streets were filled with cars. You would have thought he was having a party or going to war. I was a bit scared, since I'm used to a bit more of a covert approach. This looked like he was going for an in-your-face Neil Baggio kind of approach. I didn't see Diego anywhere, but I did see Pan out front.

"Pan, where's Diego?"

"What's it to you? You weren't even going to tell me he was alive! What's that bullshit?" There's that attitude, as usual.

"Did I do something wrong? What am I missing here? I was doing what Diego wanted me to do."

"You shouldn't have let Diego get beat up like that." Pan kept leaning into me.

"Pan, what are you talking about?" Shit, I saved him!

"You know exactly what I'm talking about.

Diego's inside!" She quickly turned and brushed me aside.

As I walked past Diego's version of Cerberus, I couldn't help but wonder what the disrespect was all about. The house was packed with people loyal to Diego. This was beginning to look more like a war than anything else. As I made my way through the sea of people, eventually getting to him, he was in his kitchen, like all great leaders are in a crisis.

"Diego, what are they doing? Rallying for a war?" I asked softly.

"No, nothing like that at all. Pan told them to lay low and enjoy the house. A select few and I will handle the business. You called her and told them to get together, remember?"

"Really? Doesn't look like a select few. And I was doing what you told me to!" He's acting different around me.

"Marie, fair point. I was going to rally the troops, but cooler heads prevailed."

"Speaking of cooler heads, Diego, what's up with Pan? She was giving me some shit." More than usual.

"She thinks you should have done more to save me. I told her that's a hard ask of anyone, but you know her. She would jump into any fight, regardless." And ruin everyone's cover.

"I guess saving your life, and perhaps your

organization, aren't enough for her," I said sarcastically.

"Don't take it personally, Marie . . . that's just how she is. You know that. Did you or your team come up with anything yet?"

"I'm waiting on a call to see if we have support or if we are to stand down. Let some other people do the heavy lifting. Either way, I'm going to at least see this shit through, one way or another."

"That's what I was thinking; let's get moving. You, Pan, and I can lay low and keep it within reason. Do you think your buddy Christian will be out there?"

"You can count on it. He's the guy looking over my shoulder right now. Do you have a more specific location for the meeting yet, so we can better plan this out?"

"Yeah, I'll shoot the specifics to you on your phone so you can share it with the necessary people. I hope we're not walking into a trap, though. I confirmed with a contact at the port that they are expecting the usual place for Andy's meetings. It's a kind of safe place for him. His uncle still owns a company that works along those docks."

"Well, if you know the way, we'll have to let you lead. Let's get Pan and head there. You guys can drive separately until we get close, then we can figure it out. The more options we have, the better if it goes south."

"Let's do it." Diego was fired up.

With Diego leading the way, we headed out. I messaged Neil and Christian with the information he had given me. Neil told me he was finishing up with Mike and just needed a few more things. He also threw in there a thumbs up plus a few money signs. I hope that means what I think it does; also, look at Neil, using emojis! While getting my mind right, listening to some guilty pleasure kind of music, the phone rang.

"Damn girl, are you jamming to some NKOTB in that ride of yours?" Shit, I forgot the Bluetooth was off.

"My bad, Neil. I forgot I had it off sync. One second . . . there we go. I like to listen to pop music, especially boy bands, when I'm getting ready for a stressful op. Not sure why, I just have forever. I have a playlist of nothing but Bieber, Timberlake, and Bellion. I know I have issues, but so do you. What's up?"

"Well, we have good news: the money transferred around and landed back in Andy's account, just like it was before you stole it. TJ made it look like he merely washed it and brought it back to his accounts, spread out over a few different business holdings, but it all adds up. Mike and the FBI are working on warrants now to arrest him tomorrow. No one knows what we did, the usual." Neil laughed.

"That's great. It's also why Mike likes using your team. They stay clean, and don't have to ask questions. What does that mean for tonight?" I quickly changed subjects.

"It means you guys are flying solo. No one wants to touch those docks—too many jurisdiction issues, and they don't want to get the military involved. As far as we know, it could just be a meeting. Mike suggested to simply watch and report. Don't engage. If you're worried about the drugs, track them, and we'll get them in the sweep-up of Andy and his holdings."

"I'll see what I can do with Diego and his right hand. Does Christian have orders to stand down?"

"Christian's orders are still the same. Protect you, be your backup, and, if possible, shoot Gaines in the leg, really close to his crotch. Okay, that last part isn't true, but it would look funny on a company memo."

"Neil, you really are one in a million. I'll do my best to get as much intel as we can and minimize contact, preferably to none." I was smiling, but felt my stomach turn.

"Sounds good. Good luck." Neil hung up, and we were on our own.

As we got within a block or two of where we were headed, Diego pulled off the road, to the side, and waved me up. When I got up there, something didn't feel right. Maybe it was just my anxiety knowing we were going in there solo.

"Hey, what's up? Everything good, Diego?"

"Have your partner meet us here. Then we can split up. I'll drive up about a mile and loop around. You two, go in from here. That way we'll have both entrances and exits covered." Diego pointed it out to me on a map.

"Is it cool if I snap a picture of that map?" I wanted to lean in and kiss him, but Pan was glaring at me.

"Let me know when he's here, and you're in position. We have a little bit of time. Andy likes to do meetings at eleven on the nose. He's routine as shit, which makes him such an easy target." Diego wasn't smiling. All business.

"How do you think I was able to get to him? Side note: We should be good on the money thing. They are working on the paperwork to pick him up tomorrow." If someone doesn't shoot him first.

"It's a start. He'll find a way to wiggle out of it just like Gaines did. Those guys are the kind of douche bags that keep surviving when none of us know why." It's because they have money and connections.

Diego took off and started his trek with Pan to get in position. Christian pulled up just a few minutes later. I forgot I still have that tracker on. My backpack is in the back of the Jeep; he probably just saw we stopped.

"I take it you were keeping tabs on me with the tracker?"

"Yeah. I saw you stopped, figured this is where we were heading in from. I'll double back a bit, park my car farther down, and work my way across the tops of those containers over there. I'll be able to keep a good eye on you. Maybe put that small tracker in your back pocket, just in case things get hairy? It's your call, though. I'm just following your lead." Christian looked amped. He's always ready for these moments.

"Not the worst idea, plus we'll have a long-range tracker on us if needed. You never know what you might need until you wish you could start over and replan your attack. This is real life, no respawn." My stomach was in knots. I'm not fearless; I just push through it.

"I know, right? I think that's a bit of bullshit, though. It makes this job so much harder."

Christian was laughing.

"Let's get after it. I just texted you a picture of the map with the location and the angle that Diego is going to take. Let me grab my camera and some personal backup. I hope it doesn't come to it, but you know it probably will."

"Exactly, Marie, we got this. We've both been in worse spots with less support. If a shoot-out happens, the security and military will show up . . . eventually!" He paused for a good ten seconds, then handed me a walkie.

"Very funny and well played. Look at you coming prepared. This will make it a bit easier to talk to each other. Good looking out."

"You really are used to going in blind, with only your wits to save you, aren't you?"

"Christian, this is the first time since my training that I had backup. I guess technically we had some backup in Santa Fe, but it was different."

On that somber note, the two of us took off sprinting in different directions. I grabbed one last thing as I took off: a fanny pack filled with a surprise. I was utilizing all my training and having a blast, using this place as my own parkour park.

We were getting closer and closer to the water's edge along the port entry when we noticed cars pulling in. You could see the lights in the distance, which changed our tactics a bit. My sprinting quickly became controlled movements, almost like a Cirque du Soleil show. I whispered to Christian, "Are you getting anything from that perch?" I couldn't see him. I was just guessing.

"You can't see me. There's no way. And yes, I can see Gaines and Andy getting out of their cars. It looks like LT is with Andy. They're walking up together. There's also a truck there, with some writing on it. I can't make it out from my angle. It almost looks like a—"

"It says Trustia. That arrogant prick isn't even hiding what he's doing. He just drove that drug right in here."

"He doesn't lack confidence, that's for sure. Wait a minute—did you notice that? Gaines's demeanor changed really quickly. Message Diego, see where they are."

I pulled out my phone while trying to keep an eye on everything and take pictures at the same time. I'm one minute away from dropping everything and looking like a rookie. I was able to message Diego, but all I got back was a picture showing him within fifty yards or so of the meeting, like an idiot. He's going to get himself caught, maybe shot or worse.

"Christian, he sent me a video, showing him within fifty yards. Looks like he's to the left of Gaines, about forty-five degrees from the front.

Can you find him, make him out?"

"I see him. He's doing a good job hiding; not sure they can see him from there, as long as he doesn't get antsy and move closer. It looks like he's filming or taking a ton of pics. He has his phone up a bit, like he's recording."

"Do you see a little Asian-looking girl around there? His first lieutenant now is Pan. She is always by his side, like in one of those mutant movies."

"You mean the X-Men movies. Hilarious. No, I don't see her anywhere. I'm going to focus on the meeting, though, no need to keep scanning. There aren't any signs of movement. They're just talking aggressively. Andy has his hands up; it looks like he's trying to calm people down."

"I need to get closer so I can hear some of this. I guess I can trust that Diego has it on video or some other form of recording."

"Stop! Don't move. LT just pulled a gun on Andy. You seeing this?"

"Yeah, he's got it pointed right at his head while Gaines is yelling at him. I can hear that all the way over here. He's calling him dumb, careless, and an idiot. I feel the same, but not sure a bullet to the head is the best option."

"No wonder LT left Diego. He's trying to take over the whole game with Gaines. Is he even smart enough for it? Your notes and feedback don't paint him as a mastermind."

"Oh, shit, I'm pretty sure LT is about to shoot him. He's tensing. He's gearing up to pull the trigger."

21

"Christian, please tell me you spotted…"

L T, with Gaines cheering him on, pulled the trigger and sent Andy's brain all over that dock. The rest of the crew that was with Andy and LT must have known this was coming. They didn't even flinch one bit. They knew they were walking him to his death. We were sitting there watching this shit go down, finding out what the next move would be. I was tired of waiting, didn't want to see those drugs make their way to the streets. With Andy out of the picture, all that money is gone from my account, but back to the city. I was a bit pissy and irrational.

I reached into my little fanny pack and grabbed the Semtex and remote detonator I had packed for backup. I was waiting to see whether the truck was actually filled with drugs. I was afraid that Gaines and LT had set this up and used an empty truck to bait Andy at the dock.

"Christian, we need to see inside that truck. Any ideas, other than being patient?"

"Marie, I don't see any options other than blowing open the door and seeing what's inside. There seems to be a pretty big lock on there."

"If you don't have any good ideas, then maybe Diego does."

"I don't think so. They just spotted him, and now they're grabbing him. He dropped the phone, though, so hopefully they don't notice."

"Shit, they have Diego and just killed Andy?! He's as good as gone. Any sign of Pan anywhere?"

"I still have nothing on her. I don't see any movement outside of the group of guys with Gaines and LT. Marie, where are you going?!"

"Get ready to start shooting."

I took off sprinting, jumped over a barricade, slid through a stack of large pipes, and kept traversing through the obstacle course in front of me. I heard my father yelling at me, demanding perfection, speed, and agility. I could hear him encouraging me, reminding me I could anything as I moved through all the obstructions with ease. As I got within twenty yards of the group, Christian started firing on Gaines and LT, causing them to scatter. He really is as good as Neil says about reading the situation from afar. A girl could get used to this kind of coverage.

They were sprinting in different directions, trying to find the shooter. I made it to the truck and they began firing on me. I made my way to LT and tackled him to the ground, quickly slipping the tracker in his back pocket. I wasn't close enough to get to Gaines. This will have to suffice. What I'm about to do is going to send everyone and everything scattering.

Up from tackling him to the ground, I took off toward the Trustia truck again. I slid under it, pressing the putty-backed explosive into the undercarriage. I continued sliding all the way toward the water's edge, hung on for dear life, and pulled the trigger. As it exploded, I dropped the detonator in the water. I had lost my fanny pack, but the gun was still holstered in my back carry.

"Marie, you're crazy, maybe as crazy as Neil! Are you okay over there?"

With my knuckles a bit torn up from the explosion, I pulled myself up, deaf as shit. I heard Christian talking to me, but I couldn't make it out. I kept asking him if he saw Diego. All I heard back were mumbles and grumbles. There were a few bodies on the ground, but it was hard to tell if they were dead or just knocked out.

I didn't see any pools of blood, but I did see that people had scrambled all over. It took me a good three minutes and gunfire with two guys that are no longer with us for my senses to come back. I know I said I wasn't going to kill anyone, but in this situation, all I cared about was staying alive and keeping Diego in one piece.

"Christian, I don't see Diego anywhere. Do you have him? Do you see him anywhere?"

"Marie, that's what I was trying to tell you. I finally found Pan. She killed him. I saw it clear as day: She shot him from the corner. I saw the muzzle flash go off, Diego go down, then I finally saw her taking off in the distance."

"Where is he? Where did you see him last?"

"Go about forty yards toward your three. He's back behind those barrels. That's where I saw him fall."

"While I'm looking for him, see if you can find Gaines or LT; I want those assholes. Focus on Gaines, though. I put my tracker on LT. We should be able to track him for a little bit before he finds it."

"On it."

I sprinted to the corner, where I found Diego, behind the barrels, with the life draining from his face. Not again, not two times in just a few weeks. I felt the first tear run down my cheek as I knelt down to him. Holding him, as he bled out on the concrete, I knew there was no chance.

"Diego, please don't go. Don't leave me."

"Marie, you and I both know this is it for me." He began to cough up blood.

"Diego, please, hang on. Just hang on a little bit. You can do this."

"Marie, I know we only knew each other a short period of time, but I really—" and just like that, he died in my arms. I gave him one last kiss, closed his eyes, and stepped back.

I don't want you to think I'm cold, but I have spent my life compartmentalizing things like this. There will come a time and a place. Right now isn't it. There are other things currently more important than my feelings for Diego.

"Christian, please tell me you spotted Gaines."

"I have his car heading out of here, with Pan in the front seat. How many double-crosses did this asshole pull off?"

"Meet me back at the Jeep and pull out your tracker. Let's get on LT at least. Maybe he'll get us back to Gaines!"

We took off running back to the car. I had no choice but to leave Diego there. I cared about him, he made me feel special, but I couldn't save him. I kept replaying it all over in my mind, what I could have done differently. Did I do this to Diego? Were my actions the reason he died? I know Christian said that Pan did it, she shot him, but I feel responsible. I feel like it's my fault he's no longer here.

We had already taken off after LT when I realized that neither of us had grabbed Diego's cell phone. I shot Neil a text and told him where it was and asked if he could try to find it. I didn't look back to check my phone for the rest of the drive. As Christian and I took off heading toward the signal, he barked out directions to me.

"Wait a minute. I know where that is. We were just there the other night when I called you. That's the place LT sent me when Diego was hurt."

"That's right, I remember. He's stopped for now, but what's the next move?"

"We don't have the firepower to go in there with guns blazing, but chances are that Gaines and the rest of the drugs are in there. I don't think it's a coincidence that we're heading back over there."

I decided to call Uncle Phil and fill him in on the night's festivities. He suggested we lay low and allow the local law enforcement and the DEA to raid the building. They could use Mike's warrant as cause to go early, that he's a flight risk, and use intelligence to claim Andy is there, though we all know that's not the case.

If we're lucky, Neil can find the phone and meet

us at Christian's place, though Christian and I realized we had left his car near the scene. Since we were told to stand down, that we had done our part, we took our salty asses back to the docks to get his car. If Neil isn't there yet, I might even go searching for the phone myself.

"Are you going to be okay, Marie? You've had a pretty rough couple of weeks. I know you didn't have a lot of time with Diego, but it was obvious you cared for him."

"It's a part of the job. We need to shut off that part of us. We need to be cold a bit."

Back at the docks, Christian got out of the car but wouldn't leave me. He kept insisting that I call Neil to see if he could get the phone before I head back in there. By now, cops and security would be all over that place. At least Neil has FBI credentials and has a chance of getting in there without too much trouble. He has a point, but I have all this restless energy. I need to do something, hit something, or sleep with something.

I know it's self-destructive behavior to think that way, but with Maria and now Diego, I feel that part of me has left. I can feel parts of my psyche and my soul disappearing. Though it might be better for the job moving forward, as a person, I'm going to be heartless. It's not a choice at this point, but it is something that I feel is taking me over. I reached out to Neil, mainly to get Christian off my back.

"Neil, any luck yet?" I was getting impatient.

"Marie, yeah, I got it. I need to talk to some people here first, see how much they have on you or Christian. Give me thirty or so minutes, and I can meet you guys back at his apartment and we can look through his phone."

"Thanks, Neil." Christian nodded to me as he heard the conversation through the car speakers.

We took off, driving in tandem back to his place. I broke off for a few minutes. I needed to clear my mind. Plus, I was mad at the world. It was a small attempt at gaining control, but it was needed. I was craving it, losing tonight, seeing Diego like that, and knowing Andy is gone.

Gaines got his way again. His drugs will get on the street. Whether through Pan or LT, he'll find a way to get someone in place down here. As I pulled up the street and parked, I could see Christian glaring at me, giving me that look of a pissed older brother, though I'm older than he is. He looked a bit judgmental, and I wasn't about to let that slide.

We walked up the stairs and into his place, knowing Neil wasn't going to be around yet. I needed to get control back in my life. I needed to dominate another person. It's what I'm good at, but lately I've been failing. Once emotion got involved, I started to slip. I wasn't about to let my feelings cloud what I did next. I grabbed Christian by the belt, kissed him, and dragged him eagerly into the bedroom. All of a sudden, I felt my phone going off. I quickly ducked into the bathroom.

"Get ready, I just need a minute." For a moment I fought checking my phone.

There was a text message from an unknown number. "I know who you are looking for, and you can meet them at the same place you first met Diego." I wasn't sure what was up with the cloak and dagger shit, but I didn't care. Then there was a second message, it was a picture with Councilman Rivers and Gaines, walking into the bar together. After everything that had happened, my adrenaline was waiting to fire. In the time I had dipped into the bathroom, I heard someone at the door, probably Neil. I quickly walked out, grabbed Christian's pants, enjoyed the view for a brief moment and threw them back at him.

"Hey Christian, get dressed, someone's here. I'll see you out there." He looked confused, for good reason.

I took off, closing the door behind me. Walking toward the front door, I heard Neil knocking and let him in. As I opened the door, he had a look on his face that made me think he was pissed at me all over again.

"Neil, what is it? Did you lose the phone?"

"No, it's not that. I just got off a call with Mike, from the FBI. We have a problem." He handed me the phone.

"If we have the phone, LT, and a track on the drugs, what's the issue? Did they see Christian or me on security footage?" I was beginning to get antsy. It had only been a brief moment since I received that text, but I was trying to play it off. I wanted to disappear. Even though I had built up trust with Neil and Christian, I was fighting the urge to fall back into my old habits of running solo.

"No, you guys are all clean. Someone called off the raid, someone powerful enough to have a judge stay the order until tomorrow."

"We know it's not Lucinda or Vanessa Clark. That was all a misdirect from Gaines's crew keeping Andy clean, since he couldn't do it himself. Who is it then?"

I had an idea.

This isn't just some throwaway. It might have failed to come up in the chaos, but Neil and his team cleared Lucinda and Vanessa. All the crumbs were put there by people working for Gaines. Pan's picture came up multiple times. More like a blurry vision of someone we assume to be her. It fits with some of the times I knew she was in those areas.

"We're pretty sure they are moving everything out of that building as we speak," he said, pissed.

"What the hell?! Let's get over there now!" Part of me wanted to redirect them.

"Marie, it's time to slow down, and focus on the next step: Diego's phone. Oh yeah, I almost forgot. Do you know a Councilman Rivers?"

"How is he involved?" I was both confused and excited.

"He was the guy who pulled strings to stop the raid. Mike said he had his fingerprints all over this."

"He's the father of the missing girl we rescued. That might explain a text I just got a minute ago."

"Were you going to say something?" Neil looked more annoyed.

"It told me to head to the bar where I first met Diego if I want to catch Gaines and Pan. At least, that's what I'm assuming. It was a bit cryptic. I know the where part for certain, but I have no idea who from."

We went back and forth, talking about what to do, as we moved out of the apartment into my car and Neil's. I led the way as they stayed back. We were in contact the whole time while Neil had TJ run a trace on the number that texted me, trying to get some information on who sent it or where they might be. It was late in downtown New Orleans, and traffic wasn't moving. I quickly pulled over, leaving the car wedged in an alley.

"Marie, what are you doing?" Christian yelled into the phone.

"I'm getting out. You know where I'm going. I'll see you two there." I had too much of every type of emotion to sit still right then.

I quickly took off, threw in my headphones, flipped up my hoodie, and turned up the volume of the music I had open on my phone. You might as why would someone even think to do something like that? Well, for starters, I just lost a man I was having feelings for, I was finally dealing with getting over killing Agent Garcia, and this kicked those emotions into high gear. I almost hooked up with Christian in a poor attempt to gain emotional control. With the bass filling my ears, my heart began to match, pumping and increasing the flow of everything to my body. Not wanting to be outdone, the adrenaline started to ramp up, giving me a turbo boost matched only in video games. I was making ease of benches, fences and even large walls as I began to treat the neighborhoods I cut through as a training course. I could hear my father once more in my ear coaching me, pushing me, with visions of Diego just hours earlier. I wanted vengeance for him, I wanted Pan, and I was going to get it.

As I made my way to the bar, I could see a commotion surrounded by customers and familiar faces I had seen with Gaines as well as the docks earlier. This is where they hide out, as they regroup before making their next move. This is what that message was about. I quickly took out my earbuds and texted Christian and Neil: "Where are you?"

22

"I'm stuck in here, on my own as usual."

Neil responded that he was getting close, and Christian was working to find a line of sight to cover us in case anything went sour. These are the stories I've heard. This is how Neil works. Christian covering him as he goes in with no plan and no idea. At least there are two of us acting on the fly. Hopefully, we don't kill each other.

I figured I could play this one of two ways: I could try and surprise them by taking people out one at a time, or I could walk up obviously. I don't think they know Neil, but they do know me. Then again, it's pretty busy and dark. I could get away with taking down a few of their crew before anyone noticed. I quickly called Neil.

"Marie, what are you about to do? I was already

walking up to the bar from the street. I'd say I won't do anything stupid, but we know my history."

"I'm going to quietly walk in, hat down and hoodie up. Then I'll start taking out guys as they notice me, or I notice them until I see Gaines or Pan. Most of them don't know you. Why don't you come to join me?"

"I'm still working on getting over there. I'll be there ASAP."

The door guy didn't even bother carding me, which made me angry. Then again, I know I don't look that young anymore. The least he can do is be nice to a lady and ask. Back to the real problem, I already recognized several guys in the crowd, trying to blend in, from my quick count. It felt weird to be in the bar now; it felt like a quiet hole-in-the-wall when I was here the first time. Now there's a late-night DJ busting it by the dance floor bar. I mean, I get it. New Orleans night life is all about what brings them in. Tuesday at seven versus after midnight on the weekend is a bit different.

I made my way to the DJ booth, tipping them with a few hundred I happened to still have on me. Threw them a kiss and a little flirting and told them to turn it up loud and ignore what happened on the floor. I gave him a few of my favorite songs and asked if he could keep it coming. Hey, this isn't the movies where the music just happens to fit perfectly. If you want a soundtrack, you have to take care of that shit yourself.

With the music pumping, this time without the restrictions of headphones, I began to work through the packed crowd mixed with henchmen. I almost made it the whole time without using that word, but I couldn't resist. This moment fits perfectly with it. The first two noticed me immediately, and I went to work on them quickly, using the butt of one's gun to knock out the other, then choking out the first. Back to my search, I worked up to the next man, smaller in stature but still, in my view, I made quick work with a chokehold, pulling him to the bathroom, where I found two more waiting for me.

As I slipped into the shadows, I could feel the tension increase in the building from the DJ turning up the bass. If I survive this shit, I'll have to find a way to tip them again. Even with the two men standing in front of me, about to cause pain for the next few days, my mind drifted in and out of thought. I was focusing on the task at hand, but I was thinking of my father, thinking of Diego and thinking of that helpful DJ.

The first guy lunged at me, almost drunk. I stepped to the side, tripping him and smashing his face into the wall. The second quickly came at me half-assed. This might be the B squad with the top-line talent guarding all the drugs or Gaines himself. It didn't take much but a few combos and some decent footwork to knock him out. My hands were pulsating more than my heart, and my knuckles starting to bleed as I left the dark hallway near the bathroom.

Out to the dance floor once more, I found three men and the frame of a small female fitting that of Pan. There is no way she was out here waiting for me, is there? Maybe she's the one who sent the message? Where is Neil? My mind was racing. I caught myself making eye contact again with the DJ when I felt the sudden burst come across my face.

"Son of . . . " That shit hurt.

Pan came out of nowhere and blindsided me. It's what I get for letting my mind wander. I know my father would be disappointed. I know Christian is trying to get a vantage point to help, but it won't do much in here. Neil is nowhere to be found. I'm stuck in here, on my own as usual.

"I can't believe you were dumb enough to fall for that shit." Oh, it was Pan all right, with burner phone and a brief message to clean up some loose ends. That's all it takes. I'm going to wipe the smirk off her face.

"How lovely, Pan. You've got me here. Now let's stop wasting time."

I charged her, trying to make the fight a close one. I've seen her scrap a few times and I know she does well when the fight is kept mostly at a distance. She's fast and has explosive moves. I need to stay inside and keep it tight like a grappler, even if it's not a strong suit of mine. When I would get close, she would fight me off, causing me to adapt. As we exchanged advances, I would go inside. Then she'd push me off while striking me. I would have to retreat and find something to maneuver around in the bar until we made our way outside. This process took a few minutes, though it felt like twenty. Exchanging blows, blaring music, a large audience and looking for help, with none in sight, I thought my only chance to survive this would be to get outside where Christian might be able to prevent my imminent death.

"There's no one to help you. No one is on Diego's side. He's gone, and you're about to be too. Just another sad story. The dead dealer's girlfriend." Pan is ice cold.

Most of the patrons stayed inside, but kept an eye on the brawl. I was outnumbered five to one. Pan was circling me with her four guards behind her as a barrier to ensure I didn't go anywhere.

Covered by the cloak of darkness, I felt I still had a chance when I could hear the roar of an engine in the background. In a voice I'm familiar with came the words "Heigh ho Chevy-O!" Like that, I heard wheels squeal, and the car come barreling down, then a quick e-brake turn into the four men as if an NFL linebacker had tackled all four at once. Neil hadn't run them over; instead, he bitch-slapped them with a car. This guy is too much sometimes.

It was then, with Pan distracted, that I got close and put her in a submission hold, but I quickly felt something sharp in my side. What the hell is that?

"Pan, it's over. Give it up!" Neil stepped out of the car.

"Are you sure? Do you even like this girl?" She has a point!

"I don't care about her! Sorry, hon. I care about Gaines! Where is he?"

"He's long gone, you know that. As for your friend here, she better let up or she's about to find out how quickly someone can die from a wound to their side." That's when I realized Pan had a blade digging into me, already working its way through a layer or two of flesh.

"I'm fine, Neil!" At least, I thought so. "Where is Gaines? You heard the man! What good is my life compared to the millions that jackass will take?" I'm all over the map, but I'm not concerned with my own well-being right now, which makes me dangerous.

"You're not dumb enough to . . . " Yeah, I am.

"Marie, what the . . . " I could hear Neil scream as I plunged the knife deeper into my side and pushed Pan away.

"Eat shit, Pan! Christian takes the shot. I know you're there!" I yelled and hoped he had one.

Suddenly I heard a loud crack fill the sky, and Pan fell back. I was already on the ground looking up, unable to move, when I heard her say, "Gaines is heading back to Detroit. He's coming for you, Neil! Watch your back!"

The pain and knife kept me lying still until I finally heard lights and sirens show up. Just like the movies, they always show up a few minutes too late.

WAKING UP IN the hospital was a great feeling. It hurt, oh did it hurt. But it felt great to be alive. I looked around, but there was no one to be found. There was no sign of clothes or a bag from someone like Neil or Christian, but that's not surprising. I would expect them to keep going after the leads for

Gaines and the case.

"Look who's finally awake." It was a nurse, coming to check my vitals.

"How long have I been here?" I could barely open my eyes, but it looked dark outside.

"Just a few days. But you gave everyone a scare. I'm not going to ask how you got that wound. Lucky for you, the surgeon had spent a few tours overseas patching up soldiers. They had seen this kind of thing before."

"I guess that is lucky."

"Oh, before I forget, there is a note for you. One of your friends left it. They stayed until they knew you were out of the woods, then they left."

"The job always comes first. I'm touched they stayed that long."

I opened the note, and it simply said,

What's lost must be found. Don't stay lost too long. You've got work to do.

— Neil

ABOUT THE AUTHOR

Charles D'Amico is an author and entrepreneur. His debut novel, *Veritas*, won the 2021 PenCraft Award for Literary Excellence in Suspense and was named a finalist for the 2021 Readers' Favorite International Book Award in the general mystery category. *Colloquium*, Book 3 in his Neil Baggio suspense series, earned second-place honors in the PenCraft Awards' mystery-sleuth category.

Charles lives with his wife and children in Amarillo, Texas, where he owns several Jimmy John's restaurants.

For more great titles from Blue Handle Publishing authors, visit BHPubs.com.

Or you can follow us on Twitter and Instagram:
@BlueHandleBooks

Our Founder Charles D'Amico
@Charles3Hats
on all platforms

<u>Other Authors on Instagram</u>

Leslie Liautaud
@author.leslie.liautaud

Jordan Reed
@author.jordan.reed

Andrew J Brandt
@WriterBrandt

Ray Franze
@TheHeightsNovel

Check out these other great titles from Blue Handle Publishing!

THE WIZARD'S BREW
By Jordan Reed

BLACK BEAR LAKE
By Leslie Liautaud

PICTURE UNAVAILABLE
By Andrew J Brandt

Get a copy now wherever you buy your books!